Chanekka Pullens Publishing Presents

# The Secrets That Lies Between:
# A Collection Of Erotic Short Stories

## By:*Whitney Sawyer*

Contact Information:

Email: WhitSawyer2016@gmail.com

The Secrets That Lies Between: A Collection Of Erotic Short Stories

© 2020 Whitney Sawyer. All Rights Reserved.

Books may be purchased in quantity and/or special sales by contacting the author by email at: WhitSawyer2016@gmail.com , with "Book Purchase" in the subject line.

ISBN: 978-1-7355910-0-1

1. Erotica

First Edition

Printed in the USA

Dedicated to:

My boys, Jaylen and ZaCari, for making me the woman I am today!
I love you both. And to my love, Justin, thank you for loving me.

I

## Acey And Drew

"Let's take a break," I said to Janelle, my best friend. "Come on. Let's walk by the park."

My name's Acey, well, Melanie, a high school senior. But the way my body was shaped, people always assumed I was older. Acey, was a nickname given to me by my family. They said it's from my father, but I've never met him. My mother never mentioned him, and I never asked. She died a year ago, so I would never be able to.

"Acey, we have a big test tomorrow. We should keep studying. I don't want to fail!" she replied.

"You won't. Come on!" I urged her.

She put on her sandals and followed me out the door. We always went to *Oakland Park,* where all the hot shots be.

"We hit the jackpot today," I told her as we walked up, sitting on the bench. All the fine guys were out playing ball.

"Acey, there he is. Go speak!" she teased.

I looked up and there stood Drew, the biggest drug dealer around. He was muscular, 6'0, with a low-cut fade. He had captivating brown eyes that weakened my body. He caught me staring, so I hurried and looked away.

"I can't! He's way older than us," I blushed. As I turned to look at him again, he was walking towards us.

"Hey, I'm Janelle," she said as soon as he approached. She didn't waste any time. "This is Acey. She thinks you're hot!" She confessed.

"Uh! Janelle!" I screeched bashfully, covering my face.

"I'm Drew," he said. "You come here often. Why haven't you ever said anything? You're shy?" He asked me.

"Me? Shy?" I asked rhetorically with a smile.

"Let me take you home," he said, grabbing my hand. I stood up and we headed to his car. "Yo, fellas! I'll catch y'all later!" He shouted to the court.

When we reached the car, he opened the door for me. A few minutes later, we pulled up to my house. He parked, exited the car, then walked around to open the door for me. He took my phone and put his number in it, as I stepped out.

"Call me," he stated, leaning in to kiss me on the forehead.

"Okay," I replied, walking away.

He remained parked, watching me, until I entered the house. I was still blushing from earlier. Before he turned off my street, I texted him, changing my life forever.

## II

Two months passed since I met Drew. Now, everyone knew me as Drew's woman. He spoiled me so much, that I literally got a gift every day. I was always popular, but now, I was the biggest name at Oakland High. Yes, I was 17 and he was a 32-year-old drug dealer. But he showed me off and he didn't care about my age. And neither did I. I loved my Drew and he loved me.

"Acey, I love that new necklace!" Janelle exclaimed, walking up to my locker.

"Thanks to Drew," I smiled, turning towards her.

"Just be careful. Don't get caught up, Acey," she warned.

As we walked outside after school, Drew was driving up. "Yo, get in," he said, pulling to the curb.

"Janelle, are you coming?" I asked, obliging his command.

"No, I'll text you later," she replied.

As soon as we pulled off, Drew asked, "Yo, what's her problem?"

"You know her," I answered, leaning over to kiss him.

"I have a surprise for you," he smiled.


When we arrived at my house, my grandma was gone to work. "Come in," I told him.

He followed me into the house, carrying a gift bag in his hand.

"Here," he said after I shut the door.

I opened it and pulled out a diamond ring. "Drew!" I gasped.

"You're my woman. You have to be labeled as such."

*Drew's Lady* was engraved around it. And trust me, I wore that title proud. I was a virgin, and he had never pressured me to have relations with him. That made me love him even more. Today, however, I felt that it was only right.

"Drew, I'm ready," I said softly.

He looked at me with his charming smile, then led me to my bedroom. "Don't worry, I'll be gentle," he comforted.

He slid me onto the bed, then began kissing my neck.

"Take your time with me," I moaned.

He unbuttoned my pants, pulled them off, along with my panties. Next, he took off my shirt, revealing my hardened nipples. He spread my legs wide and began to kiss around her. When he started flicking his tongue up and down on my pearl, I couldn't help but squeal. He placed one hand on my inner thigh, as the other caressed my nipples. After I climaxed for the first time, he came up and began to kiss me passionately. He unzipped his pants, displayed his penis, and entered in.

"Drewww!" I let out, digging my nails into his back.

His body flowed on top of me. I felt every stroke, every inch, that he was giving me. This was my first time, and I loved every minute of it. Suddenly, he pulled out, and laid back on the bed.

"Get on top," he demanded.

"On top?" I asked nervously.

"I'll teach you," he smiled.

I climbed on top and inserted him inside of me. "Ummm," I cried out, taking him in its entirety.

He held my hips, guiding me, as I began to ride back and forth. When he started licking my nipples, my nails dug into his chest. I bent down, kissed him, then rose back up. He slightly lifted my hips, encouraging me to bounce up and down. His penis penetrating deeper than before.

I felt that I was about to climax again, "Drewww, I'm about to … I'm about to …"

"Do it for me, baby," he moaned.

*BOOM!*

A part of me couldn't believe that I'd just became a woman. But I loved Drew and was willing to do anything to make him happy. As I was caught up in the moment, I slipped up and said the L word.

"Oooh, Drew, I love you!" I declared, still catching my breath.

"I love you too, Ac—"

"Acey!" a voice screamed with shock, interrupting him.

## III

"Janelle!" I yelled, pushing Drew off me. "How did you get in here?" I asked angrily, wrapping myself in the sheet.

He began to get dressed.

"You left the door open!" she shouted, standing in the door.

"I'll catch you later," he said, kissing my forehead.

As soon as I heard the front door shut, I hollered, "Janelle, I don't know what has gotten into you. But you can't go barging into someone's house like that!"

"Acey, since you've met Drew, you've changed. We don't study anymore or nothing!" she explained, stepping to me.

"Why are you giving Drew a hard time? What is the deal? You weren't like this when we first met him at the park."

"Acey," she said calmly, dropping her head. "There's something I've never told you. I know I should have."

"What?" I asked, lifting her head.

"Drew used to date my sister," she confessed.

In that moment, my heart began to race, and my eyes widened. Diamond, Janelle's older sister, was someone not to mess with. The word around town was when you broke up with her, she made your life a living hell.

"Janelle! How could you not tell me? You didn't tell her, did you?"

"I didn't have to! She saw y'all together. But I'm sorry. I should have told you!"

"Just leave please. Now!" I shouted.

At that same moment, Drew was across town.

"Drew!" a voice yelled. It was Diamond walking up to his car at the gas station.

"Yo, I told you, it's over! Leave me be!" he snapped.

"That's who you leave me for? Somebody in high school!" she screamed, approaching him.

"Back the hell up from my car, Diamond. I told you, I'm done! I've been done with by your ass."

"Drew, you better wat—"

"If you do anything to Acey, I'll kill you," he interrupted, grabbing her by the arm. He slung her away, got in his car, and drove off.

She continued to stand there. "You'll be sorry, Drew Green. You'll be sorry," she promised.

IV

A week passed since I talked to Janelle or Drew. He was calling, but I didn't pick up.

*Ringggg.*

"Hello?" I answered.

"Yo, come outside," he said.

I hung up the phone, slipped my shoes on, and went outside. When I got into the car, I sat there in silence. *Do I say the first word? Or should I let him*? I thought. Fuck it, I'll start.

"Drew, how could you!" I shouted, turning to him.

"Acey, I'm sorry. I should have told you!" he pleaded.

"Drew, do you even know what you've done? What you've started?"

"I never wanted to hurt you, Acey. I do love you."

When he said those words to me, I instantly surrendered. How could I say 'no' to love? I looked in his eyes and smiled, "I love you too, Drew."

He grabbed my face and planted the biggest kiss on me. "Come on, baby, it's shop time." He started the car, and we were on our way.

I was still known as Drew's Lady and I was still by his side. I enjoyed all the attention and love from my man. Afterwards, as we headed to the car, he paused. "Come stay with me tonight."

"Okay," I replied with a smirk, continuing to walk to the car.

Soon, we pulled up to his house. "Hold up. I got something for you," he said, reaching into a *Kays* jewelry bag.

When I opened the box, it was a pair of white diamond hoop earrings. *'Acey'* was inscribed in white gold across them.

"Drew!" I blushed, leaping over the seat, hugging him tightly. "Let's finish what we started," I whispered in his ear, nibbling on it.

He led me into his house, straight to his bedroom. He kissed and licked on my body, as we fell onto the bed.

"Do you love me, Acey?" he asked, entering me with his finger.

"I love you, Drew!" I moaned loudly.

"I love you too, Acey," he grunted.

He directed me to remove my clothes, as he did the same. Once we were naked, he flipped me over on my back. He began to plant kisses over my body. As he kissed my neck, I arched my back. He placed both hands on my hips, lifted me slightly, then slipped in.

"Yessss," I moaned out.

Our bodies were going together with the flow of his stroke. He soon turned me over and began stroking me from the back. I took his deep pounding for several minutes before I was ready to lead.

"Lay down," I told him, seductively.

He grinned, laid on his back, and relaxed. I then took his penis and locked my lips around it. I used the motion of my hands to greatly massage it, as it hardened with each suck I gave. Drew moaned and squealed, as he directed my head with his hands. The more I went up and down, the more he moaned. I continued to pleasure my man with my throat until he did the unthinkable. He busted into my mouth. I stopped, swallowed, and gave him a smile.

When we finished, we laid there, covered in sweat. Drew had his arms wrapped around my body, pulling me close. He loved me like nobody ever had before. *Drew my Drew*, I thought. Soon after, I drifted off to sleep.

*BAM!*

We jumped up from the bed with Drew's car alarm going off. We hurried, put clothes on, and ran outside. What we saw startled us, although it wasn't a surprise. There was a brick thrown through his car window.

V

Two days passed since the brick went through the window. I hadn't even heard from Drew since the morning after. I called and texted him, but he didn't reply. I was standing at my locker when I saw Janelle walking towards me.

"Acey, I'm ... I'm sorry," she stuttered.

"Janelle, it's okay. I just want my best friend back," I said.

She smiled and gave me a hug. "I'm glad to have my best friend back!" she declared, relieved.

"Janelle, I haven't heard from Drew in days," I complained.

"Acey, it's the weekend. Let's go have fun. Get your mind off Drew," she suggested. "So come on." She said, pulling me by the arm. "We're supposed to have a new teacher in history. Maybe he's cute!"


When we entered the class, there stood a gorgeous woman. The bell rung a few seconds later.

"Hello, I'm Ms. Williams, and I'm your new history teacher," she said, writing her name on the board.

She proceeded to introduce herself. Apparently, she was engaged with no kids. She then encouraged us to go around and introduce ourselves. Hours later, the bell rung for dismissal. Janelle and I stayed back to talk with Ms. Williams. She seemed to be cool.


Later that evening, Janelle and I went to *Lee Lee's Pizza*, the hangout spot on Friday's. It was always packed with music blazing through the speakers. After we ordered our pizza, as we were laughing and talking, Janelle looked up.

"Acey, is that Ms. Williams?" she asked.

I looked up. "Yes, that's her. Come on, let's go speak." We stood and walked up to her table.

"Ms. Williams, hey!" we said cheerfully in unison.

"Janelle! Acey!" she replied, surprised to see us.

"What are you doing here?" Janelle asked.

"We just came to have a bite to eat."

"We?" I asked.

"Yes, me and my fiancé." She touched the shoulder of a man who was turned around. I didn't even see him standing there at first. "Boo, I want you to meet some of my students. This is Acey and Janelle."

When her fiancé turned around my eyes shot open. My heart started pounding out of my chest. To my surprise I was looking at my man, Drew!

## VI

"Nice to meet you ladies," he said.

Janelle was stuck, looking at him, then me.

"Same to, ummm ... you," I replied numbly. "Ms. Williams, we ... we ... have to go." I muttered, turning to walk back to our table.

"Acey, I'—" Janelle began.

"No, Janelle! I know what you're going to say," I snapped.

"No, Acey. I was going to say that I'm sorry!" she replied, consoling me.

"Let's just go," I said, grabbing my purse, and running out.

The sound of me weeping broke the silence. I could not stop crying the entire ride to my house.

"Call me later," Janelle insisted as we pulled up.

"I will," I responded, stepping out.

My grandma's car was in the driveway, along with one I'd never seen. Drew was currently in the back of my mind. I was more curious as to who was in my house. I hurried to the front door, unlocked it, and entered urgently. My grandma was sitting on the couch with a stranger.

"Acey, I'm glad you're here. I want you to meet someone," she said instantly.

The man stood up and smiled. "You're even more beautiful in person," he said.

"Acey, honey, this is." She paused. "This is your father."

I stared at him with tears still in my eyes. "Daddy?" I asked in disbelief. I instantly turned, ran to my room, and slammed the door.

"Ace, just give her some time. She'll come around," his mother assured him.

He disregarded her statement and walked towards Acey's room.

*Knock. Knock.*

"Acey? Can I come in?" he asked, slowly opening the door.

"Why are you even here? You didn't want to be here!" I yelled.

"Acey, that's not tr—"

"Now, that I'm 17, you want to come into my life?" I interrupted.

"Acey, believe me! I wanted to be here for you," he pleaded. "I just couldn't. But I asked about you every day." He cried. "I'm here now. Please let me be here for you."

I looked at my father with tears in my eyes. "Oh, daddy!" I said, leaping into his arms. I had no strength to fight, so I surrendered.

Drew continued to call me all through the night.

*Ringggg.*

"What do you want!" I snapped as soon as I answered.

"Acey, I'm sorry. Come talk to me. I'm outside," he said, hanging up before I could respond.

I was hesitant, but I wanted to hear him out. I put on my hoodie, slid on my sandals, and walked outside. I had barely opened the door when I heard him.

"Acey, I'm really sor—"

"Drew! How could you?" I blurted out. "I really thought you loved me!" Tears poured down my face.

"Acey, I do. I love you. You're the one I want to be with."

"Drew, you're getting married!" I yelled, punching him.

He grabbed my hands and looked me square in the eyes. I knew he saw the hurt in me. He reached in the backseat and retrieved a gift bag.

"Here," he said, handing it to me.

"Drew, a gift isn't gone make this right," I declared.

"Open it," he requested.

I took the bag, opened it, and pulled out a framed photo of us. My tears of anger became tears of joy. "Drew!" I managed to say through the tears.

"Acey, I genuinely love you. I'll do whatever you want me to," he promised. "If you want me to leave her, I'll leave her."

"You'll do that for me?" I asked.

"Whatever you want," he replied, grabbing my face, and kissing me.

So, you know what that means ...

I stayed.

## VII

Days passed and everything was going well. Especially since I had my man by my side. Even though I was sharing him with Ms. Williams. I didn't care, that was my man, and I loved him. Monday at school, Janelle met me at my locker, snapping me back to reality.

"Whoa! That was some weekend!" she said, walking up. "What are you going to do?"

"What do you mean?" I shrugged.

"You're not going to continue to be with him after what he pul—"

"Janelle, please!" I snapped defensively. "We love each other. Now, if you're a real friend, just have my back!"

"Just be careful, Acey. Just be careful."

I closed my locker and we headed to history class.

As soon as we walked in, "Girls, can I speak with you?" Ms. Williams asked. We turned around and walked back out of the door. "Are y'all okay? It seems as though y'all were taken aback Friday."

"We're fine," I replied, failing to hide my irritation. I grabbed Janelle's hand and walked back into the classroom.

Throughout the whole class period, Ms. Williams kept glancing at me. I didn't know what her deal was, but I wished she'd stop looking at me.


After school, Drew met me around the corner. As we were driving to get something to eat, I noticed a black car following us. I couldn't see who was driving, but they followed the whole ride. I didn't think it was serious enough to mention it to Drew. So when we pulled up to the burger spot he got out without a worry in the world.

"I'll meet you in there," I told him.

When he walked in, I looked around. I didn't see the black car anymore. I got out of the car and hurried towards the restaurant. As I was about to step onto the curb, the black car flew by, almost hitting me.

Drew rushed out of the door, "Baby, are you okay?" he asked as I crashed onto the pavement.

"Drew!" I shouted as he helped me up. "I just want to go home with you."

"Okay," he replied.


Soon, we pulled up to his house. "Acey, I'm sorry," he said as we sat in the car. "Someone is trying to hurt you because of me."

"Drew, just promise me that you won't leave me," I cried.

"I promise. Look, I have to make a couple of rounds. Are you going to be okay?"

"Yes, just hurry back," I replied, stepping out of the car.


After he left, I went and laid on the bed. I opened *Pandora*, and Usher's *'You got it bad'* was playing. *I sure do*, I thought. I continued to lay there for a few minutes before I headed to the shower. As the water began flowing down my body, I started thinking about Drew. I began to caress my body, as if he stood behind me.

"Drew!" I moaned. Just as I was about to pleasure myself, the lights went out. "Drew? Is that you?" I asked loudly.

I stepped out of the shower and grabbed the towel. As I wrapped it around my body, I grabbed my phone. I turned on the flashlight, then picked up an empty flower vase that was sitting on the counter.

"Drew!" I called out again. "Come on, baby. This isn't funny." I said, stepping out of the bathroom. I heard a squeak coming from the kitchen. "Hello? Drew!"

As I was walking towards the bedroom, I heard another squeak. I stopped suddenly and gripped the vase tightly. I heard the doorknob turn and

*BAM!*

"Acey!" Drew shouted as he ducked. "What the hell?" He shrieked, flipping the light on.

"Drew! Somebody was here!" I screamed, breathing heavily.

"Calm down. Calm down," he said, hugging me.

"Don't leave again. Please don't leave me again," I begged.

"I won't," he replied.

## VIII

The next day, Janelle and I met in the bathroom. "Nelle, you have to get your sister to chill," I told her.

"Acey, I haven't even seen my sister. Nobody has," she confirmed, washing her hands.

We finished up in silence before walking to history class.


"Um, Acey, you'll be sitting up here for now on," Ms. Williams said as soon as we entered, pointing to a desk up front.

"But I always sit by Janelle," I replied.

"Not anymore."

I turned, looked at Janelle, and headed up front.

"Before we get started," she began, "I'll be passing out your graded papers." She walked around the class, placing papers face down on the desks.

After she put my paper down, I picked it up, and got pissed. "You gave me an 'F'?" I stood up so fast, the chair fell over. "I've never received an 'F' before."

"Well, maybe you should study a little harder," she smirked.

"Maybe you shouldn't be a bitch!" I snapped.

"Excuse me? What did you say?"

"You heard me! Maybe you shouldn't be a bitch!"

"Go to the office. And I'll be contacting your parents," she concluded, sitting at her desk.

I gathered my things and walked out. As soon as I was in the hallway, I texted Drew.

*I need to see you NOW!*

I sat in the office for twenty minutes before I ran out of patience. "Can I go now?" I asked.

"Go ahead. We've already contacted your grandmother. You have a parent conference tonight," the secretary said.

I stormed out, pissed. Janelle was waiting on me at my locker. "What is her deal?" I asked Janelle as I walked up.

"I don't know, Acey, maybe she knows," she whispered.

I slammed my locker door and headed out of the building.

"Acey, I'll see you tonight," the voice spoke.

When I turned around, Ms. Williams was standing there smiling. I mugged her, then ran out of the building. Drew was parked around the corner.

"Your wife-to-be got me into trouble today!" I said angrily, swinging the door open. Drew started laughing. "I don't see nothing funny!"

"Calm down. She doesn't know anything," he assured me with a kiss. "We'll go on a date tomorrow. So don't look like that." He said, rubbing my cheek.

"Drew, when are you leaving her?" I asked.

"Patience. Have patience, baby," he replied, before taking me home.


Later that evening, me and my father went to the parent conference. Ms. Williams hadn't arrived yet, so we waited outside the classroom.

"Don't worry, I'll take care of it," my father acknowledged.

"Hello, sorry I'm lat—" Ms. Williams said, turning the corner. "Ace!" She yelled before sh could finish her sentence.

"Dreya?" he shouted, completely stunned.

"Y'all know each other?" I asked my father as we walked into the classroom.

"Just good friends from a long time ago," he replied, looking at Ms. Williams.

"Please sit," she said. "Let me start off by saying that your daughter is a wonderful student. She just got a little mixed up."

"Mixed up?" I yelled. "I'm your top student. I didn't get mixed up in anything!"

"Acey!" my father shouted.

I bitterly held my tongue the remainder of the conference.

"Don't worry, I'll handle her," my father said as we concluded. "Let's go."

As we were walking out, Ms. Williams looked at me with a smirk. But when she looked at my father, there was passion in her eyes.

*I got you now, little Ms. Sunshine*, she thought, as she watched them leave.

"Daddy, you have to believe me," I said. "What is up with her anyways? Did you see the way she looked at you?"

"Look, Dreya and I, I mean, Ms. Williams, are good friends. We knew each other in the past. That's it," he explained.

"That's it?" I asked curiously.

"Honey, that's it. Now, let's go get something to eat."

After dinner, I met up with Janelle at her house. "So, my

father knows Ms. Williams!" I blurted out as we entered her bedroom.

"What?" she shouted. "How!"

"I don't know. Something about them being good friends in the past."

For the next few hours, Janelle and I hung out. She braided my hair, as we talked and laughed. I hadn't talked to Drew since earlier. So, I hadn't had the chance to update him about this newfound information. Just as I was thinking about him, I received a text from.

*I want to see you. I'll pick you up from your house.*

I read it and smiled. "I have to go," I told Janelle.

She lived around the corner from me; so it didn't take long for me to get home. When I arrived, the house appeared to be empty. As I was unlocking the door, Drew pulled up. He walked up and grabbed me from behind.

"I've missed you," he whispered.

"I've missed you too," I said.

We kissed while breathing heavy, stumbling to my bedroom. As always, he took his time with me and my body. He threw me on the bed and began kissing me from head to toe.

"I love you, Drew!" I moaned.

"I love you more, Acey!" he grunted.

It was like music to my ears. "Drew!" I moaned louder.

My bedroom door flew open, "Acey!" the deep voice yelled. "Wait, what the ... Drew?" He screeched as he turned on the light.

Drew turned around quickly and there stood my father.

"Acey! Get your ass up right now!" my father shouted.

"How dare you come barging into my room!" I screamed back.

"I'll be waiting on you two in the living room!" he said, slamming the door.

"How in the hell do you know my father?" I asked Drew.

"He was best friends with my uncle, Junior," he replied.

"Who?" I asked.

"Nothing. And I didn't know that was your daddy!" he said, putting on his shoes. "You know he's not going to let us be together, Acey."

"Drew, I love you. I want to be with you!" I assured him.

After we were both dressed, we walked to the living room.

"So this is what you do when we're not here?" he yelled.

"Dad, I'm not a little girl anymore!" I screamed.

"Drew, I think it's time for you to leave," he said as he stared at him. "And don't you ever see my daughter again!"

"You can't do that!" I proclaimed.

"Go to your room!" he demanded. I looked at Drew with tears in my eyes, then ran to my room.

"You stay the hell away from my daughter. You hear me?" he told Drew.

He looked at my father and left out.

"Don't you ever see him again! Do you hear me?" he asked, bursting through my bedroom door.

"You can't do that!" I snapped.

"Acey, I'm your father!"

"Oh, now you want to be a father to me?" I asked, rushing to him. "You've been gone my whole life. I'm 17 now, Ace!" I screamed, starring into his soul.

*SLAP!*

I inhaled deeply, surprised that he'd just hit me.

"Acey, ... I'm ... I'm ..." he stuttered.

"Just get out!" I yelled at the top of my lungs.

He turned and left without saying a word. I leaped onto my bed, balling my eyes out. I picked up my phone and called Drew.

"Hello?" he answered.

"Drew, I need to see you. He slapped me!" I cried.

"Meet me on the corner by the market," he said. "Acey, I love you."

"I love you too," I declared.

After I hung up the phone, I started to pack my bag.

*Beep. Beep.*

I stopped packing and read the text message. What I saw instantly caused my blood to boil. I finished packing quickly and stormed into the living room.

"Just a friend!" I shouted, throwing my phone at my father. "You slept with my teacher?" I rushed towards him, snatched my phone, and ran out of the house.

"Acey! Acey! Come back!" he yelled, running behind me. "Fuck!" He shouted, accepting defeat.

*Who the hell took a video of me and Dreya,* he thought.

## XI

I met Drew on the corner by the market.

"What happened?" he asked.

I was deep in thought, so I ignored his question. I'm wondering if I should tell him about my father and his fiancé. "Drew, I have to show you something," I finally said.

"What is it?" he asked.

"First, do you love me?" I inquired.

"Yes, I love you," he replied. "Now, what is it?"

I handed him my phone and showed him the video. He looked at it with anger in his eyes.

"I'm sorry, Drew," I said.

"I love you, Acey. It's okay," he stated. "We need a night to get away. Just you and me. We'll go stay downtown in the finest hotel and order room service."

We drove off and left the drama behind us.


Meanwhile, Ace was pacing around the house. He was speechlessly pissed as he picked up his phone.

*Who sent her that video,* he thought.

"Hell—"

"Why did you send that to her?" he snapped.

"Send who what, Ace? I don't know what you're talking about!"

"Where are you? We need to talk."

"I'm at home. My address is 6534 Hill Land Drive."

"I'm on my way," he said before hanging up. He grabbed his keys and rushed out of the house.

*Ringggg.*

"You have to pick up. Even if it's just to let him know you're okay," Drew suggested.

"I don't want to talk to him right now. If he can't accept us, then there's nothing to say," I replied. I hesitated to tell him this news. "Drew, I ... I need to tell you something."

"What is it?" he asked.

"I'm three days late on my cycle," I said, dropping my head. "Are you mad at me? Please don't be mad at me!" I blurted.

He suddenly slammed on the brakes. He took my hand, looked me in the eyes. "If you are, Acey, I could never be mad at you. I love you." He assured before kissing me. "I'll get you a test and we'll find out when we get to the room."

When Ace arrived at Dreya's house, he ran to the front porch. As he was about to knock, he noticed her door was slightly open. "Dreya? Dreya, are you in there?" he called out, walking in.

*Silence.*

"Yo, where are you?" he called out again. As he turned the corner in her bedroom, he saw her laying on the ground. There was a gunshot wound in her chest, "Dreya!" He screamed. He rushed to grab his phone and called 911.

Later that night, after we finished eating room service, we cuddled.

"Go ahead and go take that," he said.

I obliged and walked into the bathroom. I opened the package and peed on the stick. Afterwards, I walked into the room and sat on the bed beside Drew.

"Go look," he demanded a few minutes later.

I walked in and gingerly looked at the test. *Pregnant*. I didn't know how to feel. Should I be happy? Nervous? Afraid? I walked into the room and sat beside him.

"We're going to be parents," I said. Tears filled my eyes as I handed him the test.

He took it out of my hand, then he smiled. "I got you, Acey!" he assured me as he hugged me.

*Ringggg.*

"What?" I yelled when I answered.

"Acey! Don't hang up, honey. It's about Ms. Williams. She's dead!" my father said.

I was completely shocked. How do I tell Drew that his fiancé is dead? More importantly, how do I tell my father that his baby girl is 17 and pregnant.

When we pulled up, the police were already on the scene. My father was sitting on the side of the road with his head down.

"Daddy!" I shouted, running up to him as Drew walked over to the ambulance.

"Acey! What did I tell you about him?" he asked angrily.

"Daddy, please not here," I cried.

Drew soon approached us with tears in his eyes. "Drew, I'm … I'm so sorry," I said, hugging him.

A puzzled looked appeared on my father's face. "Acey, what's going on? How does he even know her?"

I took a deep breath. "Daddy, Ms. Williams was his fiancé."

"What? You're sleeping with my daughter while engaged!" he shouted, charging at Drew.

"Daddy, please! Not here!" I yelled. "Let's go home so we can talk." I told him. I then turned to Drew. "Meet me at my house." I kissed him before we all left the scene.

*Ringggg.*

"Janelle! Thank goodness you called," I rushed as soon as I answered.

"Acey? What's been going on? Where are you?" she asked.

"It's Ms. Williams … She's dead! I'm heading home. Meet me there in ten!"

"Acey, what is going on?" my father asked after I hung up. He pulled the car over and looked at me. "Talk now."

I inhaled deeply before I began. "Before you came, I met Drew. After we started dating, I found out Janelle's sister used to date him. She's crazy obsessed with him. I think she's the person that killed Ms. Williams!" I concluded, out of breath.

"Acey! What did you get your ass into?" he asked. "Just like your mot … Never mind, I'm here." He said, grabbing my hands.


When we pulled up to my house, Drew and Janelle were sitting outside waiting for us. When we walked in, my grandma was sitting in the living room, watching TV.

"Ace, where have you been?" she asked.

"It's been crazy tonight," he replied, following Janelle to the couch.

"Well, since everybody is here, I have something to say," I admitted. I stood up next to Drew. "Drew and I are pregnant." My heart was ramping up, but I maintained a calm composure. It was so quiet that you could hear a penny drop. "Somebody say something."

"I'm happy for you," Janelle said, standing to hug me.

My father looked at me with disappointment in his eyes. He stood up and approached me. "I'm here for you, baby girl," he stated. He then walked in his room as I watched.

"Grandma?" I said, swirling back around towards the couch. She was gone.

"You're her baby. She'll get over it," Janelle reassured.

"I love you. I got you forever," Drew promised as he kissed me.

Janelle's phone began to ring. "Hello? ... Yes, this is Janelle ... I'm sorry what? Where's my mother? ... I'm on my way!" she said loudly. She hung up the phone and rushed to the door.

"Janelle, are you okay?" I asked before she opened it.

"They found my sister! She's been hit by a car!"

## XIII

We followed Janelle to her house. When we entered, the cops were leaving out. They informed us that Diamond was in the hospital and stable.

"Janelle, I'm so sorry," I consoled her. She stepped back silently and walked into the back room. "Oh, Drew!" I said, leaping into his arms.

"It's going to be okay. Don't stress yourself out. You're pregnant with my child."

As he hugged me, I glanced outside through the window. In the back, there was a black car parked. At first, I wasn't familiar with it. I know it's not Janelle's. Then, I had a flashback to the day at the restaurant.

"Oh my God! Drew!" I screeched alarmingly.

"What?" he asked, jumping from my sudden outburst.

"That's the ... that's the car that tried to hit me!" I said.

"What are you talking about?" he asked, obvious that he forgot my near-death experience.

"Drew, that's the ca—"

"Why are you so surprised?" a voice interrupted.

I turned around and to my surprise there stood Janelle. She was holding a gun and pointing it at us.

"Janelle? What the hell are you doing?" I shouted, utterly shocked.

"Don't act surprised, Acey," she said.

"It was you? You tried to run me over?" I cried.

"Acey, Acey, you always have to be the perfect girl," she said calmly. "Ms. Popular in school. Ms. Straight 'A' student."

"Janelle! You're supposed to be m—"

"Shut up!" she snapped. "Why are you crying, Acey? I did all this for you!" She laughed.

"Janelle, just give me the gun," Drew instructed.

"And you! You couldn't just stay away," she said, pointing the gun at him. "First, you took my sister. Now, my best friend?"

"Janelle, he didn't take me. I'm still here," I promised. "Please give me the gun!"

"You left me, Acey! You stopped being my friend when he came around! And now, you're pregnant by this son of a bitch!" she screamed. "I did this all for you! I killed Ms. Williams for you! I hit my sister for you!"

"I didn't ask you to do any of that!" I clapped back.

"Well, I was being a friend. Something you forgot how to be!" she shouted, charging at me.

As we started fighting, she instantly dropped the gun. Drew ignored it completely and attempted to break us up. She scratched him, freeing herself, and leaped for the gun.

*POW!*

She fired once, hitting Drew.

"Drew! Drew! No, please! Get up!" I screamed, running over to him. As I was holding him, I couldn't stop crying. I was grateful that it was only a shoulder wound.

"Janelle, please put the gun down!" I begged.

"Oh no! I shot him!" Janelle said shocked, dropping the gun.

I hurried, grabbed my phone, and dialed '911'.


The police arrived soon after. Drew was being lifted into the ambulance, as my father pulled up.

"Acey!" he yelled, running to me.

"Daddy!" I said, falling into his arms.

"Are you okay?" he asked.

"I'll be okay."

As the cops were putting Janelle in the backseat, she screamed, "I love you, Acey. You were my best friend. I wish you didn't forget to be. You forgot to be!"

We continued to stand there, as they drove off. I wanted to go to the hospital with Drew. But what my father said sounded much better.

*Let's go home.*

XIV
The Finale

Graduation day was bittersweet. I didn't have my best friend to share the memory with. I thought back and wondered if I was that bad of a friend to her. Despite what she did, I thought about her often. Today was supposed to be one of the best days of my life. But there I was, couldn't stop crying. The guest speaker was talking, but I didn't hear a single word. My row soon stood up and walked up to the stage. It was now time to walk and get my diploma.

*Melanie Acey Jones.*

I instantly heard a wave of claps and cheers. I looked upon the crowd and saw my family looking proud. When I reached the other side of the stage, I looked up to the sky.

*This is for you ma,* I thought.

I wiped my tears and walked over to my family. They were still crying tears of joy when I approached.

"Come on. Time to take a family picture. Acey, you get in the middle," my father directed.

I stood in the middle, my father was behind me, and my grandma stood to my right. Drew was standing to the left of me. Yes, Drew was there, and he was still my man. And in my tummy, something was baking.

"Say, 'cheese'!" the cameraman instructed.

"Cheese!" we all said in unison, as they touched my belly.

I

## Acey And Drew: Birth

*I'm so over being pregnant,* I thought.

I was due at any moment. My emotions were wrecked, and my hormones were running rapid. Matters weren't made any better by the father. Drew and I had been into it for the last two weeks. I recently found out that he cheated on me! Some may call me naïve, because yes, I was surprised. Drew was still the only man I'd been with. He was still my everything. Hell, I'm pregnant with his child. But ever since *that* night, he changed.

I moved into my own apartment after graduation. Drew didn't move right in, but he did eventually. My father and my grandma helped me out every now and then. She kept telling me to move back home, but I wanted my family to work.

"Acey, leave that boy. You can always come home," she always said.

But I was home, alone. Drew hadn't been for a week. When we first moved in, we were happy. But as my pregnancy continued, he began to change. My father knew about everything and was furious. He never accepted him, only tolerated him for the baby. I was surrounded by negativity, until I met her.

*Ringggg.*

*Speak of the devil,* I thought.

"Hello?" I answered.

"Are you ready to pop?" she chuckled.

"Yesss!" I laughed.

It was my homegirl, Nikole. I met her in the waiting area at the OB/GYN. We hit it off immediately and had been friends since. She had her baby a week ago.

"How's motherhood?" I asked her.

"Great! Sleepless nights. But great overall," she replied. "Still no baby daddy?"

"Nope. I haven't heard from him in a week. It's hard to trust him ever since he cheated," I explained.

"Y'all will work it out. If anything, for the baby sake."

"How is your baby's father acting?" I asked, changing the subject.

"It's going great. Zoelle, loves her daddy and I do too," she laughed.

I've never met her baby's father and she's never met Drew. But the way she talked about him, I could tell that he was a great man.

*Beep. Beep.*

"Nikole, I'm getting another call. I'll call you back later," I said before clicking over.

"Yo! Where you at?" he asked.

"I'm home. Why haven't you been here?"

"I needed to clear my head," he replied.

"Clear your head?" I asked rhetorically. "Drew, I am about to give birth to your son any day now. And you want to clear your head?" I snapped.

"Acey, calm down," he recommended.

"Where ar ... ohhh!" I was interrupted by an intense pain. "Drew!" I shouted. I looked down and I was standing in a puddle of water.

"Acey! Acey!" he screamed.

"Ooohhh! My water broke!" I screamed, falling to the ground.

## II

The ambulance came and took me to the hospital. My heart shattered when it was time for me to start pushing and Drew was still not there.

"Acey, breathe, and push!" my grandma instructed.

"Where's Drew?" I screamed out in pain.

"Never mind him! You just breathe," my father said.

"Get ready. I need you to start pushing," the doctor said calmly.

"Please! I don't want to push without Drew!" I cried.

Then, right as I was about to push, Drew walked in. If looks could kill, Drew would be dead. My father shot a deadly stare at him.

"Acey, I'm here!" he retorted out of breath. He ran by my side, grabbed my hand, and kissed my forehead.

"One, two, three, pushhh!" Dr. Kenny directed, sitting between my legs.

"Grrrr!" I pushed as hard as I could.

"You're doing great, Acey, breathe," the nurse encouraged.

"Pushhh!" the doctor said again.

"Grrrr!" I pushed.

"We see his head! We see his head!" my grandma cheered.

"Okay, Acey, give me one more good push!" the doctor ordered.

"Grrrr!" I gave my final push.

The next second, I heard my baby crying. Tears instantly filled my eyes. I looked at Drew and he too was shedding tears of joy. He bent down and kissed me.

"You did it, baby. You did it," he said proudly.

The nurse placed my son in my arms. The love I felt for him in that instant could never be explained.

"Hey," I spoke softly to my son. "I'm your mama."

I kissed his head and held him tight. We named him after Drew. But for short, we called him DJ.

My father walked up and carefully took him out of my arms. "Hey, DJ, I'm your granddad," he said. "Acey, I'm very proud of you." He smiled, kissed DJ's forehead, then passed him to Drew.

I could see the love for his son in his eyes.

*I have my family,* I thought.


A week passed since I had DJ. I was genuinely enjoying motherhood. Drew came home and my family was complete. My grandma was my savior. She was there every day to help me. Cooking, cleaning, even running me baths. She was truly my rock. My father called every day to check on us. Although, she said that he hadn't been home in a few days.

"Acey, I forgot the ranch dressing. Do you mind going?" she asked when I walked into the kitchen.

"Not at all. They're in the room sleep," I replied. I then walked into the living room, put my shoes on, and headed out.


When I pulled up to the store, I continued to sit in the car for a few minutes. When I stepped out, I heard a voice call my name.

"Acey? Acey? Is that you?" she said.

I turned my head and there stood my girlfriend. "Nikole!" I said cheerfully.

She walked up and hugged me. "How is motherhood?" she asked.

"Great!" I smiled. "My family is complete. Where is baby Zoelle?"

"In the car with her father. Come on! I'll introduce you," she said.

She began walking to her car, a black Nissan with black tint. We walked around the back, to the driver side. She knocked on the window and it rolled down. My eyes widened and my heart began to race. I was shocked as hell by who was staring back at me.

III

"Acey, you're going to have to talk to your father eventually," Drew said.

It was a week since I'd talked to him last. He called, I just couldn't bring myself to talk to him yet. "Drew, how could he keep this from me? He's my father!"

"He is your father, Acey. And he loves you!" he replied as DJ started crying. "I'll get him." Drew stood up and walked to the nursery.

*Buzz. Buzz.*

*We need to talk. I'm coming over with Zoelle*, the text from my father read.

Drew was right, I needed to see my father. I needed to hear his side of the story. I walked to the kitchen and started on dinner.

*Ringggg.*

*Hello, this Acey. Leave your name and a brief message after the beep.*

*Beep.*

"Hey, it's Nikole. I haven't seen or heard from you. You ran from the car last week with no explanation. What's wrong? Call me back."

After I listened to it, I tossed my phone on the counter, and finished cooking.


*Knock. Knock.*

"Thank you for seeing me," my father stated when I opened the door almost two hours later.

"Sure," I said bitterly. "Come in."

I stepped aside and allowed him to pass. He was carrying the car seat with Zoelle asleep.

Drew walked out of the bedroom holding DJ. "How are you?" he asked.

"I'm good. Do you mind taking Zoelle back? I need to talk to Acey," my father replied.

"Sure," he said, grabbing the car seat.

"Acey, I know you'r—"

"Daddy! You should have told me! I'm your daughter!" I cried.

"I know, Acey! And I'm sorry. But Zoelle is my daughter too. And she's your sister."

"That girl is my age! Did you get a DNA test? How do you even know?" I asked, suspiciously.

"No, I didn't. But if that is what will make you happy, I'll get one," he replied.

"Please, do. I don't trust her," I said, hugging him.

As we pulled away from each other, he asked, "Can you watch Zoelle? I have to make a run."

"Sure, go ahead."

After he left, I walked to the bedroom. The three of them were sound asleep. Each child was on separate sides of Drew. I stared for a moment, cherishing this picture. But as I continued to look, I was startled. DJ and Zoelle looked uncannily similar.

*Am I looking at my baby sister or my son's sister?* I thought.

IV

"Thanks again for watching her," my father said, walking through the door. "Acey! Acey!"

"Huh? What?" I responded, snapping back into reality. Hours had passed, but I was still stuck in my thought.

"I said, thank you for watching Zoelle for me. Are you okay?" he asked, tilting his head.

"Yea, I'm fine. And you're welcome," I replied. "Just please, get a DNA test."

He picked up Zoelle's car seat, kissed me on my forehead, and nodded before he left out.

When I turned around, Drew was walking out of the kitchen. "Hey, baby," he said, kissing me. "I'm going to go make some runs. I'll be back soon. DJ is still asleep." He grabbed his keys and walked towards the door.

"Where are you going?" I smirked.

"What's wrong?" he asked puzzled

"Going out to cheat on me, Drew?" I asked sternly.

"Acey, I'm going to go make a few plays. I'm not on that anymore. We're a family!" he assured me. He kissed me on the lips, then left.


"Drew! Drew!" she yelled. He turned around from pumping gas and seen her walking up. "Why haven't you been to see me?"

"Yo, chill!" he silently shouted. He grabbed her arm and pulled her to the side. "I told you, I'm done with you! I have a family."

"Now, you want be a family. Did you forget that I befriended your little girlfriend? You can't run away from me or our daughter!"

Drew had started to walk away. But when he heard those words, he spun around. "What the hell are you talking about daughter?" he snapped, stepping to her.

"You know Zoelle is yours and not Ace's!"

SLAP!

Nikole instantly dropped to the ground.

"Stay the hell away from me and my family!" he said, stepping over her to get into his car.

"We are your family!" she screamed as he drove away.

V

A few hours later, Drew walked into the house.

"Where have you been?" I asked as soon as he walked in.

"It's 7 o'clock," he replied. "I've just been making plays. That's all." He walked to the couch, picked up his son, and said, "Look at Daddy's baby. Daddy loves you, son. We're going be a family forever." He kissed him on the head and rocked him to seep.

When DJ feel asleep, Drew went to lay him in his crib. He walked back into the living room. "I love you, Acey." He took my hand and stood me up.

As we were looking into each other's eyes, he smiled, and my heart melted. His smile had a powerful effect on me.

"I love you too, Drew," I said as we kissed.

"I'm sorry for everything I've done. I only want to make things right." He reached in his pocket and bent down on one knee. "I love You, Acey. You have my son, and I want to spend the rest of my life with you. Will you marry me?"

My heart began to race uncontrollably. I couldn't believe it. Drew was everything to me. He was truly the love of my life. "Yes! Yes! Drew, I will!" I screamed with tears in my eyes.

He slid the ring onto my finger, stood up, and kissed me. He grabbed my hand, led me to the bedroom, and stripped me down. He stood up, removed his clothes, then spread my legs. He climbed on top of my body and entered me.

"Drew!" I squealed.

"I love you, my future wife," he moaned.

His moan was music to my ears. After we made love, he laid behind me and wrapped his arms around my waist. He pulled me close, kissed the back of my neck, and whispered, "I love you, Acey."

"I love you too," I replied.

A few minutes later, Drew fell asleep, holding me tight. I couldn't sleep. I was so excited about being engaged to my best friend. However, I couldn't shake the thought of Zoelle.

*Maybe I'm overthinking it,* I thought.

*Buzz. Buzz.*

"Drew, you got a message," I told him. He didn't budge, just continued to snore in my ear. "I guess good love will do that to you." I joked. I continued to smile, as I picked up his phone.

*New Image Message.*

I clicked on it, not expecting to be delivered a shattered heart.

*"Hey, Daddy!"* was the bullet, and a photo of Zoelle was the gun.

## VI

"Get up! Get your ass up!" I screamed.

Before I woke him up, I removed the gun from the nightstand. He was as surprised by the Glock in his face, as I was by what I had saw. He quickly slid out of the bed.

"Acey! What the hell are you doing?" he shouted.

I threw his phone at his face with all my strength. "How could you?" I yelled. "Is this who you cheated on me with! And her baby is yours?" I cocked the gun.

He looked at the photo, and begged, "Baby, let me ... I mean ... I ..." He stuttered.

"Shut up!" I demanded. I took a deep breath. "Get your shit and get out of my house." I walked to the closet, grabbed his clothes, and threw them at him. "Get out ... Get the hell out now!"

He gathered his belongings and walked out of the room. I put the gun back in the nightstand and went to check on DJ. He was awake, so I picked him up, and walked to the living room. Drew was standing by the door, dressed.

"Acey, if you just let me explain," he begged.

"It's nothing to explain. I hope it was all worth it. Because you'll never see us again," I said calmly. I sat DJ in his playpen and turned back to Drew. "Here, you forgot this!" I took off the ring.

When I threw it at him, he finally began to cry. He looked at the ring, then at me and baby Drew.

"Get the hell out," I said.

When he left, a part of me wanted him to stay and explain. A part of me wished that there could be a reason. But there could never be.

*BAM. BAM.*

"Drew? What are you doing here?" she asked as she opened the door.

"Bitch! Didn't I say stay away from my family!" he shouted, pushing Nikole in the house.

"What? You don't want to take care of your daughter?" she asked spitefully.

He grabbed her by the throat and slammed her against the wall. "I'm not her daddy! Stop playing and leave me the hell alone," he said, releasing her. He stomped to the door and yanked it open. "Meet me at the clinic in the morning. We're getting a fucking blood test!" He yelled, slamming the door behind him.

"Who was that?" Ace asked, walking out of the bathroom, wrapping the towel around his waist.

"Nobody. It was the wrong address," she said. "Can you watch Zoelle? I have to go to the store. I want to cook your favorite tonight."

"Of course. But first, give me some." He walked up to her, grabbed her hand, and led her to the bedroom.


*Knock. Knock.*

"Smile, pretty girl," he smiled when I opened the door.

My grandma came and picked up DJ. Drew had called six times already, but I couldn't speak to him. I was feeling down, so I called my friend, Juelz.

I met Juelz at the pizzeria a few months ago. We hit it off immediately and he soon became my best friend. He was expecting his first child, so we connected about parenthood.

"He hurt me for the last time," I said as we hugged.

We walked to the couch and began talking. I already had a bottle of Hennessy and two glasses on the table.

An hour in, Juelz sat his glass down. "I love you, Acey," he said, looking in my eyes.

I leaned in and kissed him without thinking twice about it. "Wait ... Do we want go there?" I asked, pushing back.

"I've been wanting you since I met you," he declared.

I fell back on the couch and took my pants off. He pulled his pants down and climbed on top of me.

"Juelz!" I moaned.

"I love you," he moaned as he continued to pound me.

"I love you too, Juelz," I squealed.

*I can't believe I'm sleeping with my best friend,* I thought.

## VII

After we finished, we cuddled on the couch. I was looking at the ceiling in complete shock.

*How could I let this happen?* I thought.

"I really enjoyed that!" he said, sitting up.

"I enjoyed it too. But I think we made a mistake," I said. I hated to admit it, but it was true. I jumped up and started to put my clothes on.

"Acey, what's wrong?" he asked, concerned.

"Nothing. I just think we made a mistake. You have to go," I said, pointing to the door.

Juelz obliged like the gentlemen he was. Before he left, he kissed me.

After he left, I walked to my bathroom in a daze, and got in the shower. I allowed the hot water to hit my face as I cried. I couldn't shake the situation with Drew. And not to mention what just happened with Juelz. I literally stood there for twenty minutes. Afterwards, I snugged a towel around my body, and walked into my bedroom.

When I sat on the bed, my eyes averted to a picture of me and Drew. I hadn't stopped crying yet, the end nowhere in sight. Hearing my son always made me feel better, so I called my grandma.

"Hello?" she answered.

"Hey, I'm just checking on DJ. Is he okay?" I asked, snuffling.

"Of course. I just made him a bottle. Your father is feeding him in the other room with Zoelle."

*Silence.*

"Hello ... Acey? You still there?" she asked.

"Huh? Yea … Yea, I'm still here," I replied.

"Are you okay?"

"Yes, ma'am. I'm just a little tired."

"Well, get you some rest. The baby is perfectly fine with me tonight."

"Okay. Thank you, grandma," I said before ending the call.

I tossed my phone on the bed and finished drying off. I oiled my body, slid into my silk gown, and laid down.


*Knock. Knock.*

At first, I was hesitant. But then, I got up and walked to the door. I looked out of the peep hole before I said anything. A part of me was excited that he was there. But the other half was still going to play hard to get.

"What?" I said, swinging the door open.

"Acey, please just let me come in and explain," he begged.

He looked so pitiful. Bloody red eyes and dried tears on his cheeks. My heart desired him in every way. So, I had to let him in. Right?

"Acey, I messed up. I never meant to hurt you," he said, walking past me and into the house.

"Drew, you always say that!" I said, trying to remain calm. "You broke our family."

"I know and I'm sorry," he replied, grabbing my hands, and pulling me closer. The scent of his Cologne was intoxicating. How could I not forgive him? He leaned down, kissed my ear. "Let's go lay down." He released one of my hands and led us to the bedroom.

"Whoa! Drew, slow down. You're walking too fast," I said. I started feeling dizzy out of the blue.

"Acey, are you okay?" he asked.

"Yes, I'm fine. I just got too ho—"

*BAM!*

My head slammed into the wall as I went crashing down.

"Acey! Acey!" Drew shouted, reaching for his phone to dial '911'.

VIII

I was admitted into the hospital for two weeks. Drew was there every day, and I hadn't talked to Juelz since *that* night. I barely remember any of it. All I know is that I passed out, then woke up at the hospital.

"Acey, you scared me," Drew sighed.

I turned over and there he was, smiling and looking handsome. "Where's DJ?" I asked, sitting up fast in a panic.

"Calm down. Your grandma has him," he assured me, grabbing my hand. "Your father is on his way. I never want to lose you." He kissed my hand before continuing. "I ... I took a DNA test. The results came yesterday. I was waiting on you to open it."

My heart began to race, and I began breathing heavily.

"Shhh ... Please relax," he said, kissing my forehead.

He wanted me to relax! How could I? This could be my son's sister.

"Does my father know?" I asked him.

"Know what?" a voice said. My father walked in carrying flowers. "Acey, know what?" He asked again, sitting the flowers on the table.

"Nothing, daddy. We'll tell you when the time is right," I promised him. He looked at me and Drew suspiciously. "Daddy, I promise, it's nothing."

He sat down on the chair beside me, opposite of Drew. "What have they been doing to her?" he asked him.

"They ran a lot of tests on her. The doctor will be in soon."

"You scared me, baby girl," my father said, touching my forehead.

"I don't know what happened. I just collapsed."

*Ringggg.*

Drew was getting a call and stepped outside.

"Acey, if there's something wrong, tell me now," my father said.

"It's nothing."

My father casually stood and pulled a brown envelope out of his back pocket. "I got my results back. I wanted to read them with you."

My heart stopped as my father opened the envelope. He stared at the paper blankly.

"Dad, what's wrong?"

Without saying a word, he folded up the paper, then handed it to me. "I have to go," he said. He kissed me on my forehead and left out.

I opened the results, *0.001%.*

Tears poured down my face and my heart dropped. As Drew walked back into the room, I slid the results behind my pillow, and wiped my eyes. "Who was that?" I asked.

"My mama. She was checking on you," he replied, taking a sit. "Where did your daddy go?"

"Oh, he had an errand."


The doctor walked in ten minutes later. "Hello, Melanie, I'm Dr. Kurtz," he introduced.

"Everyone calls me Acey," I said.

"Okay, Acey. It seems like you gave everyone quite the scare. Now, your blood tests and your scans came back good." He paused.

"However, we gave you three pregnancy tests, and they all came back positive."

Just as he finished his statement, the door opened. Juelz walked in with roses and *Get-Well* balloons. I looked at him, he looked at Drew, and Drew looked at me. Tears began to roll down my face.

"We estimate that you're at least two weeks. Now, I'll say that you passed out due to stress. Try to take it easy," he concluded before leaving out.

"Who the hell are you?" Drew asked Juelz when the door closed.

IX

I saw Drew's mouth move, but I was numb. My body was in complete shock.

*Me pregnant again? I just had DJ,* I thought.

As I averted my eyes to Juelz, it dawned on me.

*Could he be the father?*

"Hello? Who the hell are you?" Drew asked him again.

This time I heard him loud and clear.

"I'm nobody. Just her best friend," Juelz replied.

"Oh, really? I've never heard of you," Drew said, looking at me.

"Thank you for the balloons. They're lovely," I said to Juelz with a smile. "But now is not a good time."

He walked to sit my balloons and card on the table. He then turned and headed towards the door. After he opened it, and before stepping out. "Is it..." He stopped mid-sentence and walked out.

"Is it what?" Drew yelled.

"You need to keep it down! We are in a hospital. You know?" I told him.

"I don't give a damn where we at!" he shouted. "Acey, ... Acey, look at me. Did you ... Did you sleep with that nigga?"

I dropped my head down.

"So, you did? I should break y..." he stopped himself.

Yes, I felt bad. But, I raised my head, looked at him with a puzzled look, and asked, "How can you be mad when you have cheated over and fucking over? Even while I was sitting at home pregnant with your damn child!" I cried. "Or what about this Zoelle situation?"

Without looking at me. "I get it, Acey. I do." He walked over and hugged me.

"It can't be his. It was just a one-time thing," I assured him. "Drew, I'm scared!" I confessed as tears poured down my face.

"Acey, I'm here. I'm here," he promised, squeezing me tightly.

"How can you when you have a baby with someone else!" I yelled, pushing him away. I was pissed all over again.

"What are you talking about, Acey? I haven't seen the results yet."

I looked at him, then grabbed my father's results from behind the pillow. "Here! It's not my father's baby!"

His eyes shot open before he dropped his head. He then looked up and stared at me. "Acey, I'm so ... I don't know what to say."

"You don't have to say anything. You broke us!" I yelled. I removed his ring from my finger *again* and gave it to him.

"Acey, what are you doing?" he asked, surprisingly.

"Drew I ... I don't ... I can't anymore," I cried.

"Let me fix this."

"Just go!" I screamed.


Later that night, the doctor came in. "Well, we're going to let you go. Do we need to call your husband to pick you up?"

"No. I'll call someone else," I replied.

After he left out, the nurse walked in carrying flowers. "Who are these from?" I asked her.

"I don't know. There's no name, but here's a card," she said, handing them to me.

I took the card out and it read:

*'CONGRATULATIONS STEPMOTHER TO BE. WE SHARE THE SAME BABY DADDY! BITCH!'*

Drew's results were also in the envelope.

*99.999%.*

Drew was the father.

X

"Thank you for picking me up," I said, stepping into the car.

I was heartbroken, but I tried my hardest to keep it together. Drew kept calling and obviously I refused to answer. I was still in shock that the man I loved had another baby by someone else.

When we arrived at my apartment, we sat there in silence for a minute. The silence was soon broken by the question I dreaded.

"Acey, is it?" he asked.

"Is it what, Juelz?" I replied.

He looked at me but said nothing.

*Ringggg.*

"Hello?" he answered. "I can't right now ... Because ... I'm ... I just can't!" He shouted irritably before he hung up the phone.

"Who was that?" I asked.

"Nobody. I'll call you later. I have to go," he replied, leaning over to kiss me.

I watched as he pulled off before I walked up to the front door and unlocked it.

"What are you doing here?" I asked him startled.

"Acey, I'm not leaving. We need to talk," he said.

"Talk about what? The fact that we have another baby on the way? Or the fact that you're a lying, cheating bastard!" I screamed, storming to the bedroom.

He continued to sit on the couch before he stood up and followed me. "Acey! I'm sorry. I never meant to hurt you!"

*Silence.*

"Acey ... Acey, will you just talk to me, please?" he pleaded.

"What, Drew? What is it that you want from me?"

"You, Acey! I want you!" he replied softly.

He walked up to me and grabbed my hands. He then sat me on the bed and looked into my eyes. Those sparkling brown eyes of his were my weakness, and he knew it.

"I'm sorry. I want you to be my wife," he continued, removing the ring from his pocket. "Acey, I'm sorry. Let me make it up to you."

How could I say no to him? He was the only man I'd ever loved. He started to kiss me softly, before he laid my body on the bed. He removed my bottoms, then his, before climbing on top of me. We began kissing again, as he entered me.

"I love you, Acey," he proclaimed.

"I love you too, Drew," I moaned.

One thing that I adored more than anything, was our makeup sex. After we finished, we laid in our sweat. Drew wrapped his arms around me and went to sleep.

Shortly after, I stood up, and went to the kitchen. I called my grandma to check on DJ, and to let her know that I was home. After hanging up, I saw an envelope on the table. I opened it and it was Drew's results. My eyes got big and my jaws dropped.

*0.000001%*

XI

Two weeks passed since I had read Drew's results. I hadn't mentioned it to him, and he hadn't brought it up. I didn't know who to trust or believe. But one thing was for sure, someone was lying.

"You don't have to come in," I told him.

My grandma invited us over for dinner. My father's and Nikole's cars were in the driveway when we pulled up.

"It's okay, babe. I'm with you," he replied.

When we walked in, my father and Nikole were sitting on the couch. DJ was in his swing asleep, and my grandma was in the kitchen.

*How could my father still be with her after the fact? They really have the audacity to sit here, as if nothing happened,* I thought.

"Dinner's ready. Let's go to the table," my grandma said, stepping out of the kitchen.

We all followed behind her and sat around the table. For the first few minutes, it was as quiet as a mouse. Everyone sat there in silence and ate. You could cut the tension with a knife.

"Acey, DJ is looking more and more like Drew each day," she said, breaking the silence.

"He is, grandma, isn't he," I replied, eyeing Nikole with the biggest smile on my face.

"Yea, so is Z—. Ouch!"

Nikole's remark was interrupted when my father pinched her under the table. She looked at him and he gave her a look. The silence reemerged.

This time it was Drew who broke the silence. "Dinner is very tasty tonight, Ms. Odessa."

"Acey, when do you go back to work?" My father cut in before my grandma could answer.

"Tomorrow," I replied.

"Well, just bring baby Drew right on over," my grandma asserted. "Matter of fact, he can stay the night." She smiled.

Now was the perfect time to break my news. Everyone I loved was there, and Nikole was the icing on the cake. "Everybody, I have an announcement," I said.

"What is it dear?" my grandma asked.

"Well, I was informed that we're pregnant!" I exclaimed with glee.

"Oh! Acey, that's great! Congratulations!" she said happily, standing to walk over to hug me.

My father stared blankly.

I mise of well wrap this news with a bow. "And ... I'm getting married!" I yelled, putting my ring on display.

"Oh! Acey!" my grandma cheerfully.

My father got up from the table and left out of the kitchen. Nikole stood up and followed him.

"Don't worry about him. Congratulations again you two!" She hugged Drew, then walked over and hugged me tightly. She released me and went to pick up DJ. "You're going to be a big brother!" She said to him.

My father and Nikole never came back to the dinner table, but we finished eating. Afterwards, we went to sit on the porch and embraced the moment under the stars.

*BAM!*

"How could she do this?" Ace said angrily.

"Calm down," Nikole replied.

"Marriage and another baby? How could she be so ... so ..."

"Acey, is in love. I think it's beautiful," she mocked.

"What? What did you say?" he said, grabbing her by the throat. He slung her against the wall and shouted, "I asked you to do one simple thing and you couldn't!" He began squeezing her neck tighter.

"Ace, please let me go!" she pleaded, gasping for air.

"I want them done! Do you hear me! Done!" he demanded, throwing her onto the floor. "Do whatever you have to do to break them apart. Whatever! If not, I'll kill you." He looked her dead in the eyes, slapped her face, then left out of the room.

XII

The Finale

Last night was a success in my book. I finally told my loved ones about my pregnancy and my engagement. I hadn't talked to my father, but I didn't mind giving him some space. My grandma was keeping DJ again, since it was my first day back to work. It wasn't too bad, but I was exhausted. So, I could use the rest. Drew went to play Pool with his boys, so I was home alone. Strangely, Nikole had been calling me all day.

*What can she possibly want with me?* I thought.

*Buzz. Buzz.*

"What in the hell do you want?" I finally answered.

"Acey! Please! Don't hang up!" she begged.

"What is it?" I snapped.

"I'm outside your house. Please let me in."

I walked to the window and looked out. I was hesitant at first, but I went to open the door, and waved her in.

"Thank you for seeing me," she said, stepping inside. She looked over her shoulder with fear covering her face. When she took off her large black sunglasses, she had a black eye.

"Nikole, what happened to you?" I asked, walking her to the couch.

"Acey, your father ... Your father's out of control!" she cried.

"My father?" I asked puzzled. "You're lying! Get the hell out, now!" I shouted, pointing to the door.

"Acey, you have to believe me," she begged, reaching into her purse. She removed two envelopes and handed them to me.

"What's this? Wait … Why should I even believe you? You want my man!"

"No, I don't, Acey," she began to explain. "It was all a part of your father's plan to break y'all up. Just open them."

I opened both envelopes and I was in complete shock. Although I'd previously seen Drew's results, I still didn't know what to believe. "Nikole, what's this?"

"These are the real results," she said, dropping her head. "Drew isn't my baby's father. Your father is."

She went on and on telling me how my father didn't like Drew. He didn't like how he cheated on and disrespected me.

"He made me come on to Drew. He wants y'all to break up," she said.

My heart couldn't take what I was hearing. I sat down beside her and began to cry.

*Knock. Knock.*

I dried my face and went to the door.

"I need to come in," he demanded as I opened it.

"Oh, good you're here!" he said relieved, walking up to Nikole and hugging her.

"Wait. You know her?" I asked, clearly confused.

"Acey, Juelz is my cousin," she replied.

My heart dropped to the pit of my gut. "So, you knew this plan the whole time?" I asked him.

"Acey, she … she asked m—"

*Knock. Knock.*

He was interrupted by hard knocks. I went to open the door frustrated and there stood my father.

I

## Candy And Ace


"How can we keep this a secret? You're married," Ace asked as he continued to stroke me from the back.

"I haven't told anyone," I moaned.

Ace was a 6'1, chocolate brother with dreads. He was 33-years-old and was recently released from prison. My name is Candy. I am 27-years old, brown skin, and thick in all the right places. Ace and I had been a secret for several years. The only person that knew, was my best friend. And yes, that's correct, I was married. But it was something about Ace that I couldn't let go. He treated me well and his sex game was amazing.

"Ummm, harder!" I seductively demanded.

We knew that we were playing with fire because he never wore protection. But I loved him, so it didn't matter to me. He was not the average man. He was a thug who did thuggish things and I loved everything about him. I didn't like that he hooked up with other women. But what could I say? I was married.

After we finished, he climbed in the bed, and wrapped his muscular arm around me. "I love you, Candy," he said as we drifted off to sleep.


Ace was gone when I woke up. But he had left a note on the pillow.

*I'll see you later tonight, beautiful.*

I instantly smiled as I read it.

*Ringggg.*

"Hello?" I answered, crawling out of bed.

"I love you, my beautiful Queen," he stated.

"I love you too, Junior," I replied to my husband.

"I'll see you tonight," he concluded before hanging up.


Later that night I heard the door unlock. My husband entered and walked towards me. He left the door opened, as his best friend followed behind. I didn't expect to see him again so soon.

"What's up, Candy?" he said, closing the door.

"Hey, Ace," I responded.

Yes, I'm sleeping with my husband's best friend.

## II

As Ace walked in, my eyes widened. The thought of them being best friends was one thing. But the thought of us in my bed earlier was another. It was playing over and over in my head.

"Hey, baby," I stated, hugging Junior. I noticed Ace cut his eyes at me.

"I missed you, baby," Junior declared, kissing me. He walked out the room and headed upstairs to put his bags up.

"Don't you ever disrespect me in my face again!" Ace said, grabbing my wrist.

"Ace, he's my husband. Stop it!" I silently shouted. Junior was walking back down the steps, as I turned loose from Ace. "Baby, I'm getting ready to go meet Dreya for drinks." I said, walking to him.

We kissed before I went upstairs to get ready. I felt Ace eyes following me the whole time. I loved Ace don't get me wrong, but he was the jealous type. Even though Junior was my husband, he didn't care. Disrespect was disrespect in his eyes. But I loved him, so I did whatever he asked.

Hours later, I met up with Dreya at *Club Drizzy*.

"Hey, boo!" she shouted as I walked up.

"Hey, love!" I gleefully replied.

Dreya was my best friend since middle school. I trusted her with my life, so she knew everything. We caught up a bit before I told her about Ace. About how we made love that morning, and him walking in with Junior.

"If Junior finds out, he's gone kill both of y'all!" she laughed.

"I know! What do I do? I'm in love with two men," I asked her. The whole time we talked, she was on her phone, grinning. "Who got you smiling?" I asked.

"Um, nobody," she snapped with a giggle. "Look, I gotta go. Call me tomorrow."

"Okay, boo," I replied, obviously caught off guard.


*Knock. Knock.*

"I'm coming!" shouted a voice as she skipped to the door. "Welcome home, daddy! I've missed you!"

When he walked in, she charged at him. They fell to the floor, as she began loving him down. After they finished, they laid there.

"I feel bad," the voice said. "She's my best friend."

"I can't stop this. I love you, Dreya."

"I love you too, Junior."

## III

A few months had passed since I *saw* Ace. My husband had traveled to Vegas for a business trip. Since the day he left, I had been sick. So, Ace came over to care for me.

"I still say you need to go to the doctor and see what's wrong with you," he said.

"I'll make an appointment today. I promise," I replied.

I suggested that he leave, but he wouldn't for nothing. Although, I had to admit, I loved having him around. It brought comfort when my husband was away.

"Look, I have to go make some rounds. I'll call you later."

He kissed me on my forehead before he left. I continued to lay down, trying to regain my strength. My body took a toll to the sickness.

*Buzz. Buzz*

I picked up my phone and read the text.

*Get up and go to the doctor!*

I was hesitant to oblige the command from Ace. But I took a shower, put clothes on, and headed out.

"Hey, Candy," a voice said from across the street.

"Hey, Ms. Judith."

Ms. Judith was my next-door neighbor. Not the good neighbor either, the nosey as hell neighbor.

"I saw Ace come out of your house. Isn't Junior gone? Is everything okay?" she asked.

I told you, the nosey as hell neighbor.

"Yes, he was coming to grab something for my husband." I replied, getting into my car.


I arrived at the clinic twenty minutes later. I parked, walked in, and signed my name on the waiting list.

"Candy Jones," the nurse called out moments later.

I stood and followed her to a back room. When we were in the room, I told her of my complications.

"Slip this gown on and we'll begin running tests," she instructed.

They ran a few tests, even giving me a pregnancy test. A few hours later, the doctor came in.

"Ms. Jones, ho—"

"It's Mrs. Jones. Mrs. I'm married," I interrupted.

"Oh, I'm sorry. I didn't realize. You don't have a ring on your finger," Dr. Falls replied. "Well, we have good news and bad news. The good news is that you and your husband are going to be parents. The bad news is you have tested positive for AIDS."

My eyes shot open and my heart dropped. I felt as though someone had stabbed me in my soul. I literally couldn't breathe. Dr. Falls continued talking. Everything he said was going in and out.

"I'll give you a minute," he said, exiting the room.

Tears began to fall down my face. I've only been with Ace and Junior. My heart was pounding uncontrollably. How did I tell them I had AIDS? The other thing was, who's my baby's father?

IV

"When are you going to leave her and be with me?" she asked.

"Stop it! You know I love Candy!" Ace shouted angrily. "And it's gone always be Candy! No matter what!"

"You haven't told her? Have you?"

*Silence.*

"Hello? Answer me dammit!" she snapped.

"No! I didn't tell her."

Obviously, Ace was aware that Candy was married to Junior. But just like her, he couldn't leave her alone. Ace had fallen in love with her. She was the only one that gave him exactly what he needed, plus more. Yes, he also had other women on the side. But Candy never questioned him about them, so he never brought them up. Ace was a fine man, so he had women from all around. But there was nobody like his Candy.

"I don't understand what you see in her! What can she give you that I can't?" she cried.

Ace began to get more irritated. He never discussed the different women he messed with, with anyone. But she knew how he fell about Candy. "Drop it!" he shouted.

"I can't! It's either me, or—"

Ace had enough, "Or what?" he said, grabbing her throat. "Or nothing!" He shouted as he threw her on the bed. "Look, you're not going anywhere. And you're going to continue to be here when I need you." He demanded before walking in the bathroom.

She sat on the bed crying. As she was wiping her eyes, Ace came out of the bathroom.

"What the hell is this?" Ace asked, holding up a full pack of pills.

She looked up with tears in her eyes, without saying a word.

"You haven't been taking your pills!" he shouted.

*Silence.*

"Dreya!" he yelled, throwing the box at her.

## V

It had been several weeks since I heard from Dreya. It wasn't like her to ignore my calls or texts. When I called today, she sent me straight to voicemail.

*Beep.*

*Hey, this is Dreya. Leave your name and a brief message after the beep.*

"Hey, girl. I've been calling you. I'm just making sure you're okay. Call me back. It's Candy."

*Ringggg.*

"Hello?" I answered.

"Hey, baby. It seems like I'm going to be gone another week. I'm really close to closing this deal," Junior explained.

"But we had plans," I snapped.

"Candy, don't start!" he shot back. "I'm really close to closing this. I'll see you Friday. I love you."

"I lov—"

*Click.*

The dial tone interrupted me. I still hadn't told him or Ace about my pregnancy. I definitely hadn't mentioned the AIDS. I know I need to sooner rather than later.

*Ringggg.*

"Hello?" I answered.

"Aye, it's me. Is he coming home?" Ace asked.

"No, he's staying a few more days to close out this deal," I replied.

"Okay. I'll be there later."


Hours passed before I heard the door unlock.

"Yo, Candy. Where you at?" he shouted.

"I'm in the bedroom!" I replied.

A few seconds later, Ace walked in, looking good from head to toe. I was standing there in my panties and bra. I was desirably waiting for him to come take me to bed. He began kissing me and caressing me like he'd never done before.

When we finished, he got behind me in the bed. This was something that he always did, but tonight was different. Ace grabbed me tighter and held me closer.

"Ace, are you okay?" I asked slightly concerned.

"I'm good, baby. Just promise me you'll never turn your back on me. Promise me, Candy."

"I promise, Ace. I promise," I assured him.

Now, I know what you're thinking. This was my chance to tell him. But I couldn't. I didn't want to ruin this moment. So, we drifted off to sleep.


Hours later, I set up and looked at the clock. It was 2:30 in the morning. I thought I heard a sound.

"Ace! Get up! Did you hear that?" he didn't budge. "Ace! Ace!" I said, shaking him.

"Candy, it's probably the wind. Go back to sleep," he replied, still asleep.

I laid back down and closed my eyes. He wrapped his arounds around me again.

*Click. Clack.*

"Get your ass up!" the voice whispered forcefully.

I opened my eyes and was in complete shock. A gun was pointed in my face.

"Dreya!" I screamed.

VI

"What are you doing?" I asked with a shaky voice.

"Get your ass up now!" she said.

I sat up and turned to get out of the bed. As soon as I put one foot on the floor,

*POW!*


I screamed loudly, as my eyes shot open.

"Candy! Candy!" Ace shouted, sitting up beside me. "Yo! What the hell? Are you okay?"

"Ace! Ace, I ... I ..." I stuttered, gasping for air.

"It was just a dream," he assured me. "Just lay back down and go to sleep." He said, turning back over.

I couldn't go back to sleep, so I put my robe on, and walked to the kitchen. As I poured a cup of water, my head continued to spin. I tried to figure out why I dreamed about Dreya. More so, why she would be shooting me.

I heard my alarm clock go off, so I walked back to the bedroom. When I walked in, Ace was coming out of the bathroom. He had a towel wrapped around his waist.

"You had a bad one, didn't you?" he asked.

I didn't say a word, I just looked at him.

"Yo, what the hell is your problem?" he asked, grabbing my wrist.

"Nothing! I think you should go!" I said irritably.

"Look, I have some rounds to make. Meet me at 7pm for dinner," he said. He got dressed, then left.

Soon after, I took a shower, then laid back down.

Later that night I met Ace at *Amor*, a fancy restaurant with dimmed lights. During our whole dinner, his phone was buzzing. He didn't answer and I didn't question it. He picked it up occasionally to look at it. But he'd put it right back down.

"You haven't said much tonight. What's going on?" he asked.

My head was in a million places. Do I bring up my dream? The baby? The AIDS? Hell, I was so confused, I said nothing.

"I'm going to the bathroom," he said, obviously annoyed.

He stood and went to the bathroom, leaving his phone on the table.

*Buzz.* Buzz.

*'Unknown Caller'*

"Hello?" I answered curiously.

"Baby, I know you—"

"Baby?" I shouted. "Dreya?"

"Candy!" she yelled dubiously.

I stared blankly, while holding the phone. My mind instantly went to a dark place. A few minutes later, Ace came back to the table.

"What are you looking like that for?" he asked as he approached.

I shot up, threw his phone at him, and ran out.

"Hello? Hello?" Dreya shouted.

Ace hesitantly looked at his phone, as he recognized her voice.

"Damn!" he said.

VII

A week had passed since I ran out of the restaurant. I hadn't seen or talked to Ace since then. He was blowing my phone up, but I didn't answered. How could he hurt me like that?

*My best friend?* I thought.

And she only called me once since then! I was truly devastated. Talk about karma, seeing how him and Junior were best friends. I missed him so much, I couldn't lie. But I wasn't ready to talk to him. At least Junior was coming home today. I'm glad he finally closed the deal. I was so happy for my baby.

*Ringggg.*

*Hey, this is Candy. Leave a message after the beep.*

*Beep.*

I listened to the message over and over.

*"Candy this Ace. I've been calling you. Come on, baby, talk to me, please."*

God, I missed him, but I couldn't deal. With Junior not being here, my life was incomplete without Ace.

"At least he's coming home today." I said out loud.

*Ringggg.*

"Hello?" I answered

"Hey, baby. My plane is going to be landing a little late tonight. I'll have my assistant bring me home. I love you."

"I love you too, Junior." I replied before hanging up the phone.

I picked it up numerous times, attempting to call Ace. But I couldn't.

Hours passed before I heard a knock.

"Coming!" I shouted, walking to the door.

"I had to see you. You weren't answering the phone. May I come in?" Ace asked.

"Come on," I said, allowing him to walk by me.

I shut the door behind us, and we walked to the kitchen.

"Ace, what are you doing here?" I asked.

"Candy, I had to see you! I'm sorry. I never meant to hurt you," he pleaded.

"Ace! She's my best friend! How cou—"

"Just like Junior is mine," he interrupted furiously.

My eyes widened. Did he really just throw my husband in my face?

"Candy, I love you. I'm so sorry."

He slowly walked over and hugged me. I was too angry to hesitate. He grabbed my face and began kissing me.

"Ace, wait," I said.

"Shhh," he replied.

He picked me up and carried me to the bedroom. Once we were in the bed, he began caressing my body. He started to suck on my hardened nipple, as he laid me back.

He began rubbing his hands across my other breast. "I'm so sorry, Candy."

I closed my eyes and enjoyed every minute of his pleasure. When I finally opened my eyes, his head was in between my thighs, licking all over my million-dollar crown.

In my head, I forgave him. I loved him. He made love to me like he was really sorry. Making me feel every tongue action, my legs began to shake. He locked his arms around my legs so I couldn't move. He didn't look up once, as my legs began to shake harder, like a volcano near eruption. When I did explode, my juices ran down, and he sucked up every bit.

"I love you, Candy. I'm sorry," he said again, licking his lips.

"I love you too, Ace," I replied.

We were caught in the moment, so we were blinded by what was to come.

"Candy!" a voice yelled.

We instantly hopped up and my heart dropped, as I stared at the figure standing in the door.

There stood my husband.

"Junior! Junior, wait!" I screamed while pushing Ace off me.

I ran to grab my rob, then chased after Junior. Ace put his boxers on and followed behind us.

"So, this the shit you do? When I'm out making money trying to take care of your ass?" he shouted when I walked into the living room.

"Junior, just let me explain!" I pleaded.

By this time, Ace walked into the living room.

"You're supposed to be my boy! But you're fucking my wife!" Junior screeched to Ace.

"Junior, I'm sorry. This is something that just happened," Ace said, surprisingly calm.

"And some things should never happen!" Junior said, bending down to reach in his bag.

He pulled out a gun and pointed it at Ace.

"Oh no! Junior, baby please give me the gun," I begged.

"Give me one reason why I shouldn't pull this trigger?" Junior asked.

*Knock. Knock.*

Junior continued to stand there, pointing the gun at Ace when the door opened.

"What the … Junior, what are you doing?" Dreya said as she entered.

"You have some nerve showing up at my house!" I angrily screamed at her. "Leave! Get the hell out!"

"I'm not leaving until you hear this," she replied. "Tell her, Junior!"

"Tell me what?" I asked, turning my attention to him.

"Dreya! Shut the hell up and leave!" he snapped.

"I'm not leaving until you tell her, Junior! Tell her right now!" she bellowed. "Mrs. Candy, always walking around like you're better than the next. You have a husband! Did you have to take Ace too? Junior, tell her, or I will." She bargained.

"Tell me what, Junior? What is she talking about?"

"I slept with your husband! How about that. Do you like that?" Dreya teased with a smirk.

My eyes got big and tears began to fall. "Junior, is this true?" I then turned and looked at Ace, wondering if he knew.

"Candy," Junior said, sensing my trembling anger.

I looked at Dreya and charged at her. "Awww! You little bitch!" I screamed.

As we began fighting, Ace tackled Junior. He attempted to get the gun from him.

*POW!*

# IX

## The Finale

"I love you," I said, carefully placing the flowers on his grave.

A year passed, and I still hadn't been able to accept his death. So much went on that night. Dreya fled the scene and I hadn't seen her since. My mama always told me, "Candy, you can't trust everybody." Boy was she right. But I never doubted Dreya. She was my best friend since middle school.

Ace didn't get charged with Junior's death. They ruled it self-defense since Junior pulled the gun out on him. However, a few months later, he got picked up for drug charges. Soon after, I gave birth to a healthy baby girl, Melanie Jones. My daughter looked like Ace more and more each day. That didn't stop me from thinking about my Junior. After all, we were married.

When I pulled up to the house, I got my daughter out her car seat. I checked the mail and headed inside the house. I began flipping through the mail, nothing but bills. Until I came across a letter addressed, 'Ms. Candy Jones'. It was a letter from Ace. I hadn't heard from him since that tragic night. He didn't even know about our child. I hurriedly opened it.

*My Candy,*
*Words can't describe how much I miss you. I could never show you how sorry I am about that night. Only the good Lord knows. I miss you, Candy, my Candy. I was so in love with you. I never met a woman that gave me what I needed plus more. But you did. Now, here I am now, sitting in this cell. Thinking how I should have did right by you. I know I hurt you. But it's one thing that I should have told you a long time ago. And I wish I didn't have to tell you like this. I have AIDS. I've been knowing for quite a while, but I didn't tell you. I hope you can find it in your heart to forgive me. I pray you never hold any hatred towards me. I love you.*

*Inmate Ace Jarrod Brown 486320*

I read the letter a few more times with tears in my eyes. "Ace, my Ace." I said to myself. I had learned to live with AIDS, so I wasn't too upset when I read his revelation. Afterall, it was my decision to cheat on my husband. It was unfortunate that I received this curse from it, but I also received my greatest blessing.

My daughter.

I

## Harlem And Juelz

No matter how much we knew it was wrong, we couldn't stop.

Drops of sour sweat dripped on my body, as he laid on top of me. He stroked me soft and deep. I could feel the love flowing throw my entire being. My heart was pumping so fast, I thought it was going to explode. I knew it was wrong, but I couldn't stop loving him. Even though he belonged to someone else, he was mine when I called him.

I'm Harlem Franklin, an 18-year-old senior at East Austin High School; and captain of the cheerleader squad. The guy I was loving was Juelz Talley. He too was a senior who played on the basketball team, number 15.

*Sigh.*

*I love that man,* I mentally stated.

He was 6'4, light skinned, with tattoos. He had a low fade, which drastically complimented his blinding smile. And, yes, he was in a relationship with someone else.

"Ummm," I moaned.

"Fuck, baby!" he proclaimed as he continued to enter and exit my body.

His chemistry matched mine. His moans matched mine. Everything I did, he matched.

"One day, we're going to get caught," I moaned in his ear.

"I can't stop. So, until then, who do you belong to?" he replied.

I looked in his eyes and yelled out, "You! I belong to you!"

*Climax!*

After our bodies exploded, we continued to lay there breathless.

"I love you, Juelz," I declared.

"I know you do," he replied with a smirk.

After I caught my breath. "Go shower. We have to get back to school."


On game days, we skipped 3rd period. We would go to one of our houses, make love, then go back to school in time for fourth period. It was like I was giving him strength for the games.

After we showered and got dressed, we headed back to school separately. We never left or came back together, not wanting to look suspicious. He went through the gym entrance and I came through the back of the school.

The bell rang a few minutes after I arrived to dismiss third period. I walked to my locker to retrieve my materials for my next class.

"Harlem! Where were you?" a voiced called out.

I turned and it was my best friend Bri. "Hey, Bri! I had a Doctor's appointment," I lied.

"Is everything ok—"

"Hey, baby," he said as he approached.

He walked up behind Bri, and began to hold her from behind. She then twirled around, and they began to kiss passionately.

"What did you just eat? Your mouth taste funny," Bri asked.

"I grabbed something to eat with a few of my teammates. You'll kiss me anyways," he fibbed as he kissed her again.

*Only if she knew.*

As he continued to hold her, I could feel the anger course through my veins. I couldn't let my face show it, so, I began searching for something in my locker. It was bad enough that he was doing this right in front of me. I wasn't just going stand there and watch it. I mean, technically, I couldn't get mad, he was *her* man.

"I love you, baby," he declared.

*Enough is enough!*

"Come on, Bri. We have to get ready for 4th period," I said, pulling her away from him "playfully".

"I'll text you soon," she told him, pecking him on the cheek.

The second we began walking away, she was in front of me for a few seconds. I knew that he would be watching us walk away. *Men, right?* I used that opportunity to turn around and look at him. I gave him a look that could kill.

"Watch yourself," I mouthed to him.

I then turned back around to my best friend and placed her right hand in my left.

*While my right hand held the bloody knife.*


In class, I couldn't stop having visions of him hugging her. Kissing her.

*Why? Why, did he have to do that in front of me?* I thought.

Thoughts continued to run through my head until the bell rang. I snapped back to reality instantly.

"You ready?" Bri asked, walking up to my desk.

I looked up at her with eyes of Satan for a blink of a second. I instantly caught myself and smiled at her.

"Yes. Let's go get ready for the game," I replied.

## II

Bri was a cheerleader as well. She was 5'4, with a light caramel complexion. Her hair was styled in loose curls that flowed perfectly down her sculpted jawline. We met at Cheer Tryouts our freshman year. We both made the team and we had been best friends since. Her and Juelz started dating then. He was faithful to her the whole time too!

*Until ...*

He was her knight and shining armor. She worshipped the ground he walked on. If he ever needed a passenger, she was always the one to ride. I was realistic about our situation. I knew that he loved her. I knew that she was his Cinderella. He cherished the stench from her ample perky ass.

*Supposedly.*

As soon as we walked into the gym, there he was. Standing there looking so delicious, talking to his teammates. When she saw him, she gleefully pranced over to him. As she flew into his arms, he gave me *that look*, so I just walked by them.

"While she's kissing him, she's tasting all my juices," I muttered to myself with utter satisfaction.

Yes, we were best friends, but I was a jealous bitch. I was raised as an only child to parents who had been married for twenty-three years. All my life I was given anything I wanted. I literally have a Bentley parked outside that doesn't come out until next year. My point? Is that if I wanted him to be my man, he would be my man. Period. One way or the other.

The game was lit. We were playing against our rival school, so the whole gym was packed tight! Juelz scored 33 points in this game. I told you, when he got my love, it gave him strength and power.

"Bri, are we going to the wing spot?" I asked her.

"No, I'm going with Juelz tonight," she replied cheerfully.

Her words released fire that punched me right in my chest. I literally got the breath knocked out of me. See, Juelz promised me that after games, he wouldn't let her go with him. Game day love was reserved for me. I allowed him to have her every other day. Was one day too much to ask? Granted, I knew that they were together. But that's only because I allowed them to be.

*For now.*

He walked out of the locker room with a few of his teammates. You could see every single pearly white in his mouth. He looked at Bri and lit up even more. He had never looked at me like that. Even as he entered my temple. My thoughts were unconsciously present on my face. I looked at him with a homicidal expression.

"Harlem, are you okay?" Bri asked with concern.

I mugged Juelz for five more seconds before I snapped out of it.

"Umhum. I'm alright, Queen Bri," I *joked*. "I'm tired. I'm going to just head home and shower. I've been sweating all day. Enjoy your night."

"Okay, love. Just text me later," she replied, hugging me.

As they walked away, eager to be together, I thought of how I was going to rip them apart.

III

The entire car ride home, I couldn't get the image of them two out of my mind. Trust me, I tried. I couldn't see how he could disrespect me like that. These thoughts caused me to literally see fire. Hate and jealousy began to emerge more and more.

"Does he not know who the hell I am? I'm Harlem! He does not want to see that side of me!" I said to myself angrily.

This was the second time that I drove by his house. Both of their cars were in the driveway. His parents were gone for the week, that much I knew. The only light that was on in the house was in his bedroom. I sat there for at least 30 minutes.

"He can't be doing this to me!" I screamed, punching the steering wheel. "He just made love to me!" I peeled off down the street. "Okay, Harlem. Get it together. Get it together." I self-demanded.

The thought of him touching and kissing her, sent the devil to my heart. I hit the brakes so hard, I slammed my face into the steering wheel. I instantly tasted blood, and I smiled. I turned my car around and headed back to his house. My reasoning told me to just go home. But my blind love and hate commanded me to go back.

Such a thin line it is.

It was a little after midnight when I pulled back up to his house. All the lights were now off. I sat there for a few minutes before opening the door. I glanced around to make sure the street was clear. Once I was sure that it was safe, I walked around to the back of his house. I knew exactly where they kept the spare key.

Again, I looked around to make sure nobody was around. I unlocked the back door and crept in silently.

I walked through the kitchen and made my way to the staircase. The night lights that lined the stairwell were the perfect guide. I tiptoed up the stairs and walked to his bedroom door. I peeked in and saw them sleeping so peacefully. He was laying on his back and she was facing the other direction.

"She can't work it like me. He doesn't even cuddle with her. He doesn't love her. He loves me," I convinced myself. I entered the room and walked on his side of the bed. As I stared at him lying there, I smiled. "Look at my man." I said silently.

I started rubbing his chest, before moving my hands to his mighty sidekick. I bent down and kissed *him*. I then moved towards his face and kissed him on the lips.

His eyes instantly shot open. "Harlem?" he whispered. "What the fuck are you doing here?"

I didn't answer. Instead, I looked over at her. She didn't move, but I knew that Bri was a hard sleeper. She could sleep through World War III. I then returned my focus on my man.

"Don't you want me, Juelz?" I asked him.

He stared at me. "Harlem, you know I do. But we can't ... we ..."

Before he could finish his sentence, my clothes were off. I went back *down* on him and enclosed *him* in my mouth. As I was moving my head up and down, I put two of my fingers in my mouth. I started to rub my clitoris with my saliva in a circular motion before I entered myself. I enjoyed myself, as he enjoyed me for a few more seconds. After I was certain that we were both ready, I climbed on top of him. I started riding him like never before. Slow and deep. I covered his mouth so she wouldn't hear, but his forbidden moans were trying to escape. I reached down and grabbed my panties to stuff in his mouth. I kissed him. I could tell on his face that he was loving every bit of it. I looked over at her again with the devil's grin on my face. I then turned back to Juelz and leaned down, while I was still riding him.

"She can't do you like me. Can she?" I whispered in his ear.

He shook his head "no".

The harder I rode, the more he moved my hips back and forth. Sweat began to pour down his face and I was loving every moment of it.

*Climax!*

After we both exploded, I climbed off him. He looked at me, still in disbelief.

"See you tomorrow?" I smiled.

I grabbed my clothes and walked out. Before I left, I took my panties, and stuck them in the pocket of his jacket; without him seeing.

*That's going be a lovely surprise,* I thought as I walked out the room.

## IV

The next day at school, Bri was at my locker waiting for me.

"What did you do after the game?" she asked.

"Oh, nothing I just went home," I said.

Even though I wanted to tell her, "Bitch, I rode your man! While you were laying there!" But I didn't. It was just a matter of time until she found out about us. Then, I would have my man.

*Ringggg.*

Bri went her way and I went mine. Before I headed to class, I searched for my man. I hadn't seen him since school started. I walked into the gym and there he was. When he saw me, his eyes widened, and he smirked. I walked over and right passed him. I went up to his homeboy, and I felt his eyes watching me. I flirted with him and giggled for a few minutes. I knew Juelz didn't like me talking to nobody else. My punishment was usually rough sex.

"Harlem!" he called out.

The devil's grin instantly appeared on my face. When I turned around, he was walking towards me. He pulled my arm and lead me back to the locker room.

"Did you enjoy the show?" I asked him.

"What the hell is wrong with you?" he asked, gripping my neck. "First, the bullshit you pulled last night. Now, you all over Tip. Keep playing with me, Harlem. I promise you; I'll break you—"

Before he could get out another word, I jerked away.

"You not gone do shit! You enjoyed last night, that's why you didn't stop me," I snapped. "Bri can't do you like me, Juelz, stop playing."

"You have to chill. You're making it harder than it has to be," he said.

I walked over to him. "Am I?"

We starred into each other eyes. I grabbed his hand and put it up my skirt, rubbing my thighs.

"Am I worth the sacrifice?" I asked. He moved his hand to my love box, making me wetter. "Kiss me, Juelz." I instructed.

He looked me in my eyes and planted a wet kiss on me. He looked at me again. "You're worth every sacrifice."

He turned me around and bent me over the coach's desk.

See, he was my man when I wanted him to be. I got him with no questions asked. I was poison for him. But the way he handled my body, he knew I was not going anywhere. He then pushed me against the wall, entered me again, and began stroking. The best part about this, was that nobody knew. The more I yelled his name, the harder he went.

Right before I was about to climax, Juelz stopped, turned my head around, and asked, "You gone calm down now?"

I was mad that he stopped, but I answered, "Yes."

He continued to stroke me until we both came. I pulled my skirt down, as he pulled up his pants. I gave him a kiss, then walked out of the coach's office in the locker room.

"Lord, help me," he said as he walked out, the door closing behind him.

I walked back over and started talking to Tip again. I looked back at Juelz, licked my lips, and smiled.

They had just started to play a game when she walked in, and shouted, "Juelz!"

I looked up and there was Bri, storming in there with his jacket.

"Whose are these!" she cried. She took my panties out of his pocket and threw them at his face.

"Wait, huh?" he said puzzled. "I ... I don't know!"

Bri threw his jacket and ran out the gym. He looked at me and mugged before he ran after her.

*Surprise, surprise, surprise.*

V

"Get the hell up now!" he shouted.

I was caught off guard when Juelz popped up in my face. I looked at him and slightly grinned. He snatched my arm, pulling me off the bleachers. He practically dragged me into the coach's office.

"What was that?" he yelled. "Is that the shit you're pulling now?"

*Silence.*

"Answer me!" he screamed.

*Slap!*

I didn't flinch, just continued to stand there in silence.

"Harlem, I can't … I can't do this anymore. We're done." He walked out of the office, leaving me there.

My heart started pumping furiously. Anger filled my body and hate was taking over.

"How can he do this to me!" I yelled, knocking everything off the desk.

I stormed out of the office, straight to my locker. He was at Bri's locker, trying to explain, but she wasn't listening.

"Harlem!" she called out. "Give me a ride home, please." She said, walking up to my locker.

"Sure," I replied.

Juelz mugged me and walked off.


That night, I let Bri stay with me. She cried all night, and I was enjoying every moment of it. But I listened to her still, as a *friend* should.

"Leave him, Bri," I suggested.

I had to fill her head up with bullshit. He was mine and I'm not going let nobody, and I do mean nobody, have him. He belonged to me.

"I love him, Harlem," she cried.

Juelz blew up her phone all night long. Every time he called, I convinced her not to answer. See, Bri was soft and weak minded. I knew if I kept getting in her head, she would leave him alone for good.

"I just don't understand. Harlem, I ... I haven't started ..." she hesitated.

I looked at her. "Started what?" I asked.

"My period," she bellowed, dropping her head.

It was like a bullet shot through my heart. He told me that they used condoms. How could he do her the way he did me? The more she talked, the more I hated her. She couldn't have a baby! Not by my man.

"Well, Bri, I guess we need to get you a test and see," I said, comforting her.

She hugged me tightly and continued to cry.

*Now, I have to get rid of the baby. Let the Devil Games begin.*

VI

Later that night, Bri was asleep in my room. I laid on the couch with a racing mind. To hear that she could have been pregnant by my man really got to me. Well, he was her man, but damnit he was mine too. A voice was playing over and over in my head. It was telling me to go get the knife and kill her ass. It could be that simple, no Bri, and no baby. I walked to my room and looked in at her. She was sleeping so peacefully. Once I even walked in there with the knife and held it to her throat.

How did I become so obsessed like this? We weren't supposed to be anything but a good fuck. But the way he handled my body, I couldn't resist falling in love. I loved everything about him. From the tattoos that covered his body; to the way he handled the ball. Thinking about him made me yearn to see him.

*Beep.*

I walked into the room and grabbed her phone. There was a text from him.

*Meet me at your house,* I replied.

I kissed my best friend on her forehead and headed out to see our man.

When I pulled up to his house, twenty minutes later, the living room light was on. In my head, the evil bitch was out. But I knew I had to be the lovely Harlem to get through the door. He was expecting someone, so he left the door unlocked.

"Harlem!" he yelled as I walked through the door.

"Wait, Juelz! Before you say anything, let me explain," I said, rushing to him.

"I thought I said I didn't want to see you anymore," he replied, pushing me away.

He grabbed my arm and pulled me towards the door. If I didn't do something right then, I could had lost him forever.

"Wait! I'm ... I'm ... pregnant!" I yelled.

He stopped dead in his tracks and spun around. He looked at me deeply. "You're what?"

"I didn't know how to tell you. I know if I'd texted or called, you wouldn't have picked up. I had to see you."

I busted into tears and he hugged me. Feeling his arms around me and smelling his Cologne, took my breath away. I knew that it was Bri who was pregnant, not me. But I had to say something to keep my man.

"Did you tell her?" he asked, continuing to hug me.

"NO! She doesn't know." I replied.

I stepped back from his embrace and grabbed his hand. I led him to the couch, pushed him down, and removed his pants. I stood in front of him, then removed my clothes. I happily hopped on top and began riding him.

He held my hips and caressed my nipples in his mouth.

"Yesss!" I moaned.

I got my man back. As usual, we climaxed and cuddled on the couch in silence. I kissed him on the lips, got dressed, then left.


Driving back home, I couldn't stop smiling. I'm happy that I got my man back. When I got home, Bri was still sleep. I went straight to the bathroom and took a shower. As I washed myself, I could still smell him on me.

*I must get rid of that baby,* I thought.

As soon as I opened the bathroom door, I was startled.

"Where you been?" a voice asked.

## VII

"Whew! You scared me," I stated with relief. "How did you get in here?"

"Your momma let me in. I thought we were going out tonight," Chris said. He was Juelz best friend and teammate.

"We were. But something came up. We can watch a movie if you want."

Now, I know what you may be thinking. And yes, I was sleeping with my best friend's boyfriend and his best friend. Neither of them knew about the other, although I was with Chris first. I really liked him at first, I still did. But I loved Juelz.

After I put on my pajamas, we went downstairs, and sat on the couch. I put *Acrimony* by Tyler Perry into the DVD. I was absolutely submerged into the movie. At that moment, I was Taraji. I understood her and I knew exactly how she felt. We were the muthafuckin' devil's together. The more I watched, the angrier I got. These bitches were trying to take from us, what belonged to us. But like her, I wasn't going to let Bri stand in my way.

When I woke up the next morning, Chris was gone.

"My appointment is at 11:30 at the clinic," she said, walking into the living room.

"Okay," I smiled.

We went to my room, got dressed, then headed to clinic.

"Harlem, are you okay? You haven't said anything since we got in the car," she asked.

"I'm fine. Why do you ask?" I replied.

"Because you're driving 60mph. Are you trying to kill us?" she asked concerned.

When we arrived at the clinic, we waited for 45 minutes. They called her back, gave her a pregnancy test, and we waited for the results. We sat there in silence the whole time.

Ten minutes later, the doctor walked in. "The test came back positive. You're pregnant," he said.

I saw fire when I heard those words and my devil horns emerged.

He continued, "You're actually going on three months."

We looked at each other and she didn't look surprised. So many thoughts instantly rushed into my head. The most important being, *'did she know this whole time?'* If so, how could she not tell me? Does she not trust me? I felt betrayed, and I never wanted to kill her so badly.

"Thank you, doctor. Can you give us a minute?" I asked.

When he left out, Bri broke down, and cried, "Harlem, how am I going tell Juelz? I told him I was taking my pills."

"Three muthafuckin' months! You kept this from me?" I shouted, walking out.

Even though I was fucking Juelz, I still had to play it off. Bri continued to sit there, deep in thought. She pondered how she was going to tell the father.

VIII

The car ride was silent. After I dropped her off, I instantly texted Juelz. He agreed to me at the gym. When I walked in, he was playing ball. As I walked to the bleachers, he followed me.

"What's wrong?" he asked concerned.

I lifted my head up and looked in his eyes. "Nothing. I just missed you so much. I had to see you," I lied.

All the while, I couldn't stop thinking of Bri being three months pregnant. I had to figure out who the fuck this bitch was pregnant by.

"Juelz, do you love me?" I asked.

He nodded, grabbed my face, then kissed me. "Harlem, not only do I love you. I'm in love with you," he confessed. "You're my drug. I can't stop."

"What about Bri?"

He turned away. "I'm in love with both of you. I can't let either of you go."

I instantly saw fire. "You're not supposed to be in love with her ass!" I snapped.

*Slap!*

All I remember is the muthafuckin' devil coming out of my soul. I was yelling, screaming, and swinging. I blacked out.

"Harlem! Harlem! Calm down, please!" he begged.

He tried frantically to grab me, but I was uncontrollable at that point. Eventually, he tackled me, and pinned me on the ground.

"Stop it! It's you that I love. I want to be with you!" He kissed me, attempting to calm my soul.

I took a deep breath and looked in his eyes. "You sure?" I asked.

"Yes. I'm sure it's you."

"You'll do anything for me?"

He nodded, then kissed me. "Anything."

"Get rid of her," I snapped, before walking out.


When I got home, I called, and texted Bri. She didn't reply which was unusual. I began to daydream about plotting the perfect murder before I dosed off.


*Ignore.*

"Juelz! What the hell is this?" a voice called out. "Is this what you do?"

She threw her phone at him. He sat up in the bed and picked up it up. His eyes widened. He was looking at a picture of him on top of Harlem, kissing in the gym. He then looked up at Bri, tears filled her eyes.

"Baby! It's not what you think!" Juelz said, leaping out of the bed. "She got sick. I was trying to help her."

He soon realized that he was set up. Harlem had bullshitted him once again. But he did love her, and she was his drug.

"Juelz. There's something I have to tell you," Bri said. "I'm … I'm pregnant!"

Juelz eyes widened, as if he'd just seen a ghost. His mind went back to Harlem telling him the same thing. He believed that he was the father of Harlem's baby. But he doubted Bri. Although they were together, they hadn't been that intimate in the last few months. He had slept with Harlem more than he had with her recently.

"I'm just a couple of weeks," she lied.

How could she tell Juelz that she was sleeping with someone else?

The next day, we all had practice at the gym in preparation for tomorrow's game. Bri barely said three words to me all day. *What does she know?* I thought. It's not like her not to say anything to me. At first, I was a little concerned. She was my best friend. But my concern soon faded. Every time I turned around, she was staring at Chris. I felt the devil coming out.

"No, Harlem. Don't explode. Keep calm." I repeated this to myself over and over.

But there was no controlling her. I looked over at Chris, who was on his phone smiling. I then glanced over at Bri, who was doing the same thing.

"Well … well … well … What do we have here?" I said. "I have to get Chris's phone."

"Hey, love. What are we doing later?" I smiled, walking up to him.

"Whatever you want to do," he replied, grabbing my waist.

"I can't find my phone. Let me see yours to call mine," I said, holding my hand out.

When he handed it to me, I went straight to his texts. I scrolled to Bri's name in his messages. It took me two seconds to discover the bullet. It shot right through me.

"Here you go, my love," I said, handing him his phone. "Meet me at the park at 6pm," I whispered before I walked away.

When I turned around, Bri and I locked eyes. That prompted me to turn back around, kiss Chris, and leave the gym.


Later that evening, I pulled up to the park. When I arrived, he wasn't there yet. When I saw his car pull up, I instantly saw fire. When he parked, I exited my vehicle, and got into his. As soon as I got in, I climbed on top of him. We began kissing, as I unzipped his pants. I proceeded to do what I did best. I could tell he was loving it, his eyes rolling to the back of his head. I grinded on him slowly and moved my hips back and forth. All the while, he licked around my nipples and played with them in his mouth. The more I rode, the more he moaned. But now, I've had enough. My mind flashed to the texts between him and Bri.

"I love you," she told him, and he loved her too.

"You're the best thing I've ever had," he declared to her.

*No, bitch! Harlem is the best your ass will ever have!* I thought.

As he was kissing on my neck, I reached inside my purse. "You love it, Chris?" I asked.

"Yesss," he moaned.

*BAM!*

I struck him in the head repeatedly.

"So, why do you love her!" I screamed, beating him.

I began laughing and I blacked out. The devil had won again. I bashed him at least 15 times before I climbed off him.

"Bri, bitch, you're next," I said to myself, covered in his blood.

I grabbed my belongings and rushed out of his car. I didn't check to see if he was breathing, I just had to get out of there.

X

When I got home, I ran straight to the shower. The image of me riding Chris came to my mind. Then the image of me bashing him replayed. Before I rinsed off all his blood, I scooped some into my nail, and put it into my mouth. *He had to die. And so does she.* I desperately tried to force the thought out of my mind. But seeing her sleeping with *both* of my men, then have the audacity to get pregnant... *Fuck, she's here.* And all I could see was fire. If I had any idea that she was sleeping with Chris, while she slept the other night, I probably would have killed her then.

*Better late than never.*


"Come in!" he shouted, sipping Hennessey on the couch.

"Hey, my King," she said, walking into the living room.

"What's up, baby?" he replied.

"I've missed you so much," Bri said, pulling on his arms, getting him to stand.

He was already feeling the Hennessey, and all he wanted was sex. He desired Harlem, but since Bri was there, he had to settle. When they entered the bedroom, Bri pushed him onto the bed.

"Let's play a little game. Shall we?" she said, taking a pair of handcuffs out her bag.

"Whatever you want to do, baby," he replied drunkenly.

Bri handcuffed each hand to the bedrail. She then stripped his pants and boxers. Afterwards, she took off her clothes, climbed on top of him, and asked, "Do you like this, baby?" as she inserted him into her.

"Yesss. I love it, Harlem. I love it!" he declared in a daze, definitely feeling his liquor.

*I knew you were sleeping with that bitch!* she thought, continuing to ride him.

Simultaneously, she leaned over and removed a butcher knife from her bag.

"So, you want to me to be Harlem?" she growled.

BAM!

"The fuck!" he screamed, twisting to toss her off him. "Bitch! What did you do that for?"

He then realized that he was handcuffed and couldn't move.

"You want Harlem? Huh?" she said. "Where is your Harlem now?" She yelled, raising the knife to stab him again.

*Click. Clack.*

"Bitch, don't move. Or I will put a bullet in your fucking head," the voice threatened.

# XI

## The Finale

"Put the knife down, now! Before I put one in you!" I yelled.

Bri dropped the knife, and I ran over to check on Juelz. "Dial '911'! He needs help!" I shouted, continuing to point the gun at her.

"This is what you do to me? You're supposed to be my best friend!" she yelled, picking up the phone.

I found the keys and unlocked the handcuffs. "Baby, are you okay?" I asked, kissing him.

He looked at me surprised. "Harlem? What are you doing here? Why do you have that gun?" he asked, going in and out in a daze.

"I came to ... I saved you! That bitch was going to kill you," I explained.

"Don't believe her, Juelz! She's crazy! Look, she's holding me at gun point!" she yelled.

"Shut up! She's lying, baby. Believe me! The baby she's carrying isn't even yours!"

"She's lying! It's yours," Bri said, looking at Juelz.

"Bitch, say another word and I'm popping your ass," I threatened her, cocking my gun. "Juelz, believe me. She was fucking Chris! It's Chris's baby. Not yours!"

"You little bitchhh!" Bri screamed, leaping off the bed, attacking me.

The gun flew out of my hand, as we began to fight. Juelz was still on the bed, bleeding out. We fell to the ground, wrestling for the gun.

*POW!*

"Ahhh! She shot me! She shot me, Juelz!" I cried, holding my arm.

"Bri! Put the gun down!" he pleaded with all of his might.

"You want me to put the gun down?" she asked him, pointing the gun at Juelz. "You've been fucking my best friend and you want me to put the gun down!"

"Bri, please. It wasn't ... I mean, I never meant ... I'm sorry! I'm so sorry!" Juelz said. "I never meant to hurt you." He cried.

"I gave you my heart! But it wasn't good enough. I knew you were fucking her! Y'all were skipping school together. Missing at the same time. I put all that shit together. It could have been anybody, Juelz! You chose my best friend." She looked at me, crying on the ground, holding my arm. "And she's right, it's Chris's baby, not yours!"

"You bitch!" he yelled, trying to reach for her. But he was too weak.

"I'm the bitch? But she's going to be the dead bitch!" she said, pointing the gun towards me.

As I looked up at Bri, I saw a shadow in the door.

*POW! POW!*

I

## Jenny, Juelz, And Harlem

"The doctor will be in to talk to you momentarily," the nurse said before walking out.

As I was getting dressed, I couldn't help but admire myself in the mirror. Tattoos covered my arms and my breasts perked up perfectly. I hadn't seen the love of my life in eight years. But I knew when I seen him, he wouldn't be able to resist me. *It's time I become Mrs. Talley. I've waited so long,* I thought, smiling in the mirror.

*Knock. Knock.*

"Harlem, it's Dr. Simpson. Are you dressed?" he asked, before opening the door.

"One second!" I replied, grabbing my shirt. "Come in!" I shouted, sliding it on.

"Are you ready to go home?" he asked with a wide smile.

"Of course! I have to get to my husband," I blushed.

"What husband, Harlem?" he asked, writing notes in his file.

He knew that she wasn't married, but he allowed her to express her delusions. It was better than getting her upset. "Well, Harlem, we're going to put you on probation for a week. Your live-in supervisor is Jenny. She will document your behavior and progress. If she feels that you're capable of unsupervised living, you'll be released. Any questions?"

"Nope. It's pretty-straight forward. I've been waiting for this day for eight years."

"The car is ready to take us home, Harlem," Jenny said, walking into the room, and grabbing my bags.

"Take care, Harlem. I'll see you in a week," Dr. Simpson stated, hugging me.

"Let's go, sweetheart," Jenny said.

"You can go ahead. I'll be right out," I responded.

After she left out, I walked to the mirror and smiled, "Okay, Harlem. It's show time. I have to get rid of Jenny, get my husband, and live life. It's time for me to become, Mrs. Talley."

I kissed the mirror, then went to confront my greatest obstacle.

## II

"Harlem, you will love this neighborhood," Jenny said. "It's nice and quiet. We have a pool in the back, feel free to use it. I want you to feel right at home."

I nodded. It was heartbreaking; knowing that she would have to die soon. But I couldn't allow anything, or anybody to stand in my way. It was time for me to be happy and I couldn't do that without Juelz.

Soon, we pulled into a gated neighborhood. Big beautiful houses lined the streets. Minutes later, we pulled up to a luxurious brick house. I could only imagine what the inside looked like.

"We're here," she said, pulling into the garage. "Someone will come get your bags. Let me show you the house."

When she opened the door, it took my breath away. The inside was gorgeous. I couldn't lie, my excitement soon morphed into anxiety. She gave me a tour, which lasted ten minutes.

When it concluded, Jenny said, "Come on. Let me show you where you'll be sleeping." We walked down a spiral staircase. I followed her to the guest bedroom downstairs by the pool. "This is your room. I hope you like it."

"This is beautiful," I said, mesmerized by the grand paintings and the view of the pool. "Do you live here alone?"

"Oh no, I live here with my fiancé," she said, holding out her arm, revealing a beautiful diamond ring. "The wedding is in two months."

"I know the feeling," I smiled. "I can't wait to marry my soulmate. What's your fiancés name, Jenny?"

"His name i—"

"Ms. Bakestale, you have a call," a servant interrupted.

"Well, I must take this call. You'll meet him tonight at dinner," she said. "Now, shower and get settled in. Dinner is at 7pm."

After I shut the door behind her, I began unpacking. *It was a shame she wouldn't be able to enjoy her marriage.* Once I unpacked, I walked into the bathroom, and stripped down.

"Alexa, play *'While We're Young'* by Jhene Aiko."

As it began to blast through the speakers, I turned the water on. When I stepped into the shower, the hot water stung my body. The average person would have recoiled, but I embraced the pain.

As I washed up, I began to think of him. I removed the showerhead, turned up the pressure, then moved it down my body. When I reached *her*, I sat on the seat, and inserted three fingers inside of myself. I held the showerhead to my clitoris and began riding my fingers. Thinking of him, I was satisfied almost instantly.

"Mmm!" I moaned.

*Knock. Knock.*

"Ms. Harlem, dinner will be ready in five minutes," Mildred, a servant, called out.

"Thank you!" I replied. I stood up, finished showering, and got dressed.


"So, what is she like?" he asked, kissing Jenny.

"Aww, baby, she's amazing," Jenny replied. "A little thrown off. She says she's getting married. But she's single. We're keeping an eye on her, so be cautious."

"Good to know. Where is she?" he asked, sitting at the table.

"She's coming," Mildred said. "Should I serve dinner?"

"No, we should wai— aww! Here she is," Jenny said when I walked into the kitchen. "Juelz, this is my patient. Harlem, meet my fiancé, Juelz."

Juelz eyes shot open, as he stared his past in the face.

III

We both became stuck in each other's eyes, like a deer in headlights.

"Harlem, are you okay?" Jenny asked. "You look like you've just seen a ghost."

Rage and anger emerged, the devil inside tried to escape. "I'm fine, sorry. I was admiring how good looking your fiancé is. It's like I know him," I said.

"Well, thank you. Now, let us sit, and eat dinner. We don't want this delicious meal to go to waste," Jenny said, walking to the table.

I couldn't take my eyes off him. I couldn't believe it had been eight years. He was much more handsome than he was on that bloody night. *Juelz, my Juelz. What is he doing with this white bitch? He should be with a Black Queen. Me, I'm his Queen. Not her,* I thought.

"So, Harlem, are you from here?" he asked, taking a sip of wine.

I wanted to say, "Duh, Bitch! Hello, we used to fuck!" But I just smiled. "Why yes, I am. I grew up here and went to East Austin High. I was a cheerleader."

"Really? Juelz was the star basketball player in high school," Jenny said, eating her side salad.

"He must have been good," I said.

"Mmm. Mildred, this food is wonderful," Juelz said to the servant.

"Is everything good for you, Harlem?" Jenny asked.

"Yes, it couldn't be better," I told her. I took a few more bites. "Well, if you two would excuse me. I'm going to go finish unpacking.

Thank you for the meal, Mildred." I stood from the table, carrying my glass of wine.

*Smash.*

I threw the glass against the wall as soon as I shut the door. I could feel the heat coming from my soul. My inner bitch was coming out, and this time, I wasn't going to stop her.

"What is he doing with her? He's mine! All mine! He loves me!" I yelled.

The guestroom was a good distance from the kitchen. So, I was comfortable that they couldn't hear me. I went and sat on the bed, rocking back and forth. I was losing it. *I hate her! She must die.* The voices in my head grew louder. They were telling me that I had to kill her, and I was listening. I stood up, walked to my bag, and removed a razor. I sat down, raised my sleeve, revealing the scars from cutting.

"Juelz can't marry her! It's me! Me! Me!"

I moved the razor to my arm, intending on cutting over my scars, but I was interrupted.

*Knock. Knock.*

"Can we talk?" he asked, as I opened the door.

## IV

"Where's your wife to be?" I asked him, closing the door behind him.

"She's asleep and keep your voice down," he replied.

I sat on the corner of my bed. I wanted to slap the shit out of him more than I wanted to fuck him. As he stood over me, I looked up, and into his beautiful hazel eyes.

"Harlem, I'm ... I'm sorry," he said.

"You're sorry?" I mocked. "I love you. I've killed bitches for you. Spent years locked up like I'm some animal. And all you have to say is 'I'm sorry'?" I yelled.

"Keep your voice down! She may hear you," he said.

"Good! Maybe I should just go tell her," I said, standing up.

"Go tell her what?" he asked, pushing me back onto the bed. "Look, Harlem, whatever we had going on, it's over. That was way back in high school. I'm with Jenny now. She's going to be my wife."

I stood up, looking into his eyes. "You don't want to go there with me, Juelz. You know I can and will be the devil in this house."

*Slap!*

"Stop it, Harlem! It's not happening anymore!" he snapped, throwing me on the bed, and walking out.

*That's what you think,* I thought.

Later that night, the house was quiet as everyone slept. Evil thoughts continued to control my mind. Plotting to kill the bitch was starting to bring me joy. I walked to the kitchen, poured a glass of water, then headed back to my room. As I passed the living room, I saw Juelz sleeping on the couch. I took a sip of water, then hesitated for one second. But that's all it took.

As I walked to the couch, I walked along the wall, examining their photos. My first thought? *I'm not impressed.* As I approached him, I was extremely astonished. His body had more tattoos than I remembered. He was worth the wait, which was now over. There was an empty bottle of Hennessy on the table. *Same old Juelz.* I thought.

I rubbed my hand across his face, waking him.

"What are you doing?" he asked, sitting up. "If she wakes up we'r—"

"Shhh," I interrupted, putting my finger over his lips.

I dropped to my knees and unzipped his pants. He was already aroused and ready to go. I put my hair in a ponytail, then began to pleasure him. I looked up at him and his head was hanging back.

"Harlemmm!" he moaned, as I bobbed my head up and down.

Then, I did what I did best. I mounted him and began to ride. He moved my hips back and forth.

"Don't you miss me?" I moaned, bouncing up and down.

"Yesss. But it's wr …" He was silenced by our climax. "We can't do this anymore." He said, breathing heavily.

But I knew Juelz like a book, and I could have him wrapped around my fingers. Just like I did in high school.

"Okay," I replied. I got off him, got dressed, and walked backed to my room. "Oh! Mildred, I didn't see you!" I said, startled when I turned the corner.

"Ms. Harlem! I … I … I was just headed to the kitchen," she stuttered, walking away.

*What the fuck did she see?* I wondered.

V

"Good morning, Harlem. Would you like some breakfast?" Jenny asked as I walked into the kitchen.

"Sure, thank you," I replied, walking to the table. "Good morning, Mildred." I smiled.

She didn't reply, only nodded with a forced smile. *She's acting weird. She must have seen us. Now, I have to k—.* My thoughts were interrupted by his intoxicating scent. Before he turned the corner, I could smell him.

"Good morning, everyone," he said, walking up to Jenny.

He leaned down and kissed her on the forehead. I simply smiled, successfully masking my true hatred.

"Good morning, my love," Jenny said to him, sipping a cup of joe.

"And what has Ms. Mildred prepared for us this morning?" he asked, pulling out his chair.

She cautiously placed each of us a plate in front of us. "Ms. Jenny, may I be excused? If there's nothing else either of you need?" Mildred asked, ignoring me completely.

"Of course. We're fine, thank you. Breakfast is good," Jenny replied.

"What's her problem?" I snapped, when she closed the patio door.

"I don't know. She's been quiet all morning. She said she has to talk to me about something important. I hope she's okay," Jenny said.

*Crack!*

"Harlem? Are you okay?" Jenny asked, rushing over to me.

I shattered the glass of orange juice in my hand. "Oh! I'm sorry!" I said as my hand bled.

Jenny ran to the sink to wet a towel. Juelz walked over to check on me.

"You enjoy me last night?" I asked him.

"Look, last night I was drunk. It won't happen again. Understand? She's going to be my wife. Stop your shit, Harlem," he said calmly.

"You know when you grab me, it gives me a rush," I said. "Either do what I say, or your little wife-to-be will know about little ol' me. Oh! I love the sound of that, 'Your little wife-to-be will know all about little ol' me'. Do you really want me to kill her, Juelz?"

"Look, bitch! I told you it ov—"

"Wrap your hand with this," Jenny said, entering the kitchen with a wet towel. She examined my hand. When she was confident that it wasn't too deep. "There's a First Aid kit in your bathroom. Once the bleeding stops, I'll have Mildred come bandage you up."

"Okay, thank you." I replied, standing from the table.

"Are you two getting to know each other?" Jenny asked, taking her seat.

"You have no idea," I replied. "Well, if you two would excuse me. I need to go get cleaned up." I left the kitchen and walked to the guestroom.


"I don't think it's good idea for her to be here anymore," Juelz said when Harlem left.

"Wait, why?" Jenny asked.

"Something about her isn't right," he claimed.

"Look, I know she's a little off. We just have to work with her. Have patience, she'll come around," she explained.

Juelz shrugged it off and stood from the table. He kissed Jenny. "I'll see you for dinner tonight. Work awaits me."

"I love you, my love. Everything is going to be okay. Have a great day." Jenny smiled, and he went on his way.

*Knock. Knock.*

"Come in!" I shouted from the bathroom.

Jenny peeked her head in. "I have to go into town. Mildred is here if you need her. Do you need me to pick you up anything?"

"No, thank you. I think I'm going to take a dip in the pool," I replied, walking out of the bathroom.

"Enjoy. It's pretty out," she said, before closing the door behind her.

I changed into my two piece and headed to the pool. I laid on a beach chair and tanned for almost an hour. It felt so good, but I soon decided to get into the water. Twenty minutes later, as I was getting out of the pool, I saw Mildred. She was wiping down the pool side tables. I dried off and went back to tanning, closing my eyes.

"I know what you did last night," she said.

When I opened my eyes, Mildred was standing over me.

"Excuse me?" I said, standing up.

"Bitch, I seen you all over him. I'm telling Ms. Jenny when she comes back," she threatened.

"You didn't see a damn thing! And it's your best bet to keep it that way," I snapped.

"You don't scare me, Harlem. I know what I saw and I'm telling her," she said, before turning to walk away.

I stood up and grabbed a rock from the pool side. "Ahhh!" I yelled out, hitting her in the back of the head.

She crashed to the ground, then I climbed on top of her. I began to smash her head with the rock repeatedly. Once her breathing was faint, I pushed her into the pool. If anything, it would look like an accident.

I hurried to my room, took a shower, and got dressed. *I told her to stay out of it,* I thought.

"She made me do it," I convinced myself, before leaving the house.

## VI

That night when I returned home, police cars, and an ambulance were there. *They must have found the bitch. Well, it's time to put on a show,* I thought.

"Harlem! Thank goodness you're okay!" Jenny sighed, as I walked through the door.

"What's going on? What happened?" I asked.

"It's Mildred! I came home, and she wa ... she's dead!" she cried, hysterically in my arms.

"What happened?" I asked an officer, while I successfully forced tears.

"It appears that she had an accident by the pool," she said. "We have a few questions that we need to ask you."

"Sure. Anything you need. I'm here to help," I replied.

I peered into the kitchen and saw Juelz. He mugged and anger filled his eyes. He looked as though he knew, but he wouldn't say anything.

"When did you see her last?" the officer asked, opening her notepad.

"Around 2pm. I went shopping to replace a glass I broke this morning. She was cleaning the kitchen we I left," I answered, handing Jenny the shopping bag.

"Oh, Harlem. You didn't have to. Thank you," she sniffled.

"Sure, no problem," I told her. "Officer, is there anything else?"

"That's all for now. If we have any more questions, we'll give you a call," the officer responded.

"Bitch! What did you do?" Juelz asked, as I walked into the kitchen. He grabbed my arm and threw me against the wall.

"Whatever do you mean?" I teased, yanking my arm away.

"I know you, Harlem. What did you do to Mildred and why?" he asked, putting his hands around my neck.

I gave him an evil grin, then he let me go.

"Don't worry about what you *think* I did. Soon, it'll be just us. Jenny will be out the picture too," I promised him with a smile.

"Bitch! If you think about doing anything to her, I—"

"You'll what?" I cut him off, stepping to him "You'll get killed like her?" I laughed.

"Harlem, this has to stop. There's nothing between us anymore," he said, backing away from me.

"Yes, there is! And there will be until I say otherwise!" I declared, walking out of the kitchen.


Dinner was quiet that night. Benzo, another servant, prepared dinner. Everyone looked at each other and ate in silence.

Just as we were finishing, and dessert was being served, Jenny spoke, "Harlem, have you contacted your husband since you've been out?" She had to keep notes on her and her progress, or lack of. As she asked questions, she wrote in her notepad.

"I see my husband every day," I replied.

"Oh, you do?" Jenny asked surprised, taking notes.

"Jenny, do you ever fear that someone will steal something from you?" I asked, twirling the knife I had in my hand.

"What kind of things?" she asked as she stopped writing and looked up.

"You know. Your house, your cars, your man?"

"Excuse me?" Jenny replied, laughing it off.

"You see, Jenny, I see my husband every day. In this house," I said.

She began writing again.

"Baby, that's enough for tonight. Let's finish dessert so we can go to bed. It's been a long day," Juelz said.

It soon got back quiet. But I wasn't done.

"Jenny, do you know why I haven't pursued anything with my husband?" I asked, staring at her.

"No, Harlem, why?"

"Because it's something standing in my way."

"What's standing in your way, Harlem? Talk to me. What's standing in your way?"

Juelz eyes shot open, and I could see his heart beating out of his chest.

*BAM!*

"You!" I screamed, stabbing the knife into the table.

They both dropped their utensils and stared at me. Fear and confusion covered Jenny's face, as anger covered Juelz's.

"Excuse me, please. No dessert for me." I said, standing from the table, and leaving the kitchen.

## VII

"What was that about?" Jenny asked suspiciously, jumping up from her chair. She began pacing back and forth. "I need to call Dr. Simp—"

"I should have told you," Juelz spoke softly, dropping his head.

"Told me what?" Jenny groaned, stopping in her tracks.

"I'm ... I'm the husband that she refers to."

"What ... What do you mean?" she asked, walking closer to him, fueled by anger.

"Baby, I know Harlem. We went to the same high school. I was ... I mean, I'm the reason ..." he hesitated.

"The reason what, Juelz? What are you saying?" she asked, practically holding her breath. She knew of Harlem's past and the reason she was locked up.

"That killing happened at my house. We had an intimate relationship," he confessed.

Jenny couldn't believe her ears, as she cried hysterically. "What! Why didn't ... I don't und ..." she began to hyperventilate. "So, I'm next?" She managed to ask.

"No, baby. I love you. I won't let anything happen to you," he replied. "I love you. I haven't touched that girl. Well ..."

"Well, what?" she asked, thinking that it couldn't get any worse.

"Nothing," he lied. "Call Dr. Simpson, now. She has to go. She's dangerous and I know what she's capable of."

"Juelz, right now, I just need you to get your shit and go!" Jenny snapped.

"What?" he asked, stepping back to look at her.

"Just go! Now!" she shouted.

He walked to the door, then turned back to her. "You're going to be sorry." He grabbed his keys before leaving out.


Later that night, Jenny couldn't sleep. She paced around her bedroom, contemplating Juelz's suggestion, to call the doctor. *I'll just talk to her*, she thought.


*Knock. Knock.*

"Harlem, can I come in?" Jenny asked, opening the door.

I was sitting on the bed, anticipating her arrival.

"Harlem, talk to me. Do you really think Juelz is your husband?"

I scooted to the end of the bed, then looked her in the eyes. "Jenny, do you know what you have walked into?" I asked.

Fear reflected on her face, but she just as quickly suppressed it. "No, Harlem. Talk to me and let me kn—"

"Let you know what, Jenny!" I snapped. "The way you're going to die? Or the way I'm going to fuck your husband again!"

Jenny's eyes widened, and she refused to back down. "You're not taking shit, Harlem! Because he's not yours!" she proclaimed.

I smiled, stood up, then walked to her. "Oh, he's mine. And if you knew what was best for you, you'd get the fuck out."

"Harlem, you're sick. Let me help you," Jenny begged.

"I can be the real motherfucking devil. I don't think that's who you want to meet."

Jenny stared at me for a few seconds, before walking out.

After she closed the door, she continued to stand there, as tears began to fall.

"I have to get this bitch out my house," she declared. She rushed to her room and called Dr. Simpson. "Dr. Simpson, it's Jenny. Please give me a call back. It's very important."

After she left the message, she walked to the bathroom.


Unbeknownst to her, I was listening outside her door. *So, she's trying to send me back. I guess I'll have to get to him first,* I thought.

VIII

*Smash!*

"Ahhhhhh!" I screamed as the vase crashed against the wall. I walked to the bed and threw everything on it to the floor. "Okay, calm down." I repeated that to myself, while taking deep breaths. "She thinks she can get rid of me? Well, she has another thing coming. I guess it's time I have a visit with the doctor." I said, grabbing my car keys.

Jenny paced around her room, trying to figure out her next step. Her wrecked nerves caused her body to shake uncontrollably. She had dealt with patients like this before, and she knew what they could be capable of. In that moment she realized that she would feel much safer if Juelz were there. She called him numerous times, but he didn't pick up.

*Maybe if I go talk to her, she'll open up*, she thought. "Come on, Jenny. You know her kind. But if she think she's taking what's mine, she has another thing coming," she concluded, walking out of the room.

*Knock. Knock.*

"Harlem, can we talk?" she asked, unaware that nobody was there.

*Knock. Knock.*

"Harlem. Harlem, are you in here?" Jenny asked, turning the doorknob, entering the room.

Her eyes widened as she looked upon her guest room. It had been destroyed. She looked around and spotted Harlem's little black book on the nightstand. She grabbed it, sat on the bed, then opened it. As she flipped through it, her mouth dropped. The doodles and entries she saw startled her. She knew that Harlem was obsessed with Juelz. But she didn't realize that she was *madly* in love with him. And that is the worst kind of love. Jenny closed the book and left out the room.


The hot water was hitting every angle of her body. She continued to think about what she should do next. Her mind then transitioned to Juelz. How she should have listened to him. How much she loved him and didn't want to lose him. She soon stepped out the shower and walked in her bedroom.

"Juelz, what are you doing here?" she asked, containing her shock and joy.

"I couldn't let you face her alone, Jenny. I know her and she's crazy," he replied, sitting on the corner of the bed.

"I know and I'm sorry I didn't listen to you," she said.

"Where is she?"

"I don't know. I went to talk to her, but she was gone," she replied, walking to him.

As she stood in front of him, he began rubbing her thighs. When he reached her love box, he began moving his hand back and forth. "I'm sorry," she said, as he laid her on the bed.

He opened her towel, took his clothes off, and climbed on top of her. He pushed her legs back and they made sweet love. Twenty minutes later, they both climaxed. As they drifted off to sleep, they failed to realize the red flashing light behind the plant.


*Knock. Knock.*

"Come in!" the voice called out. "Harlem! What a nice surprise. What are you doing here?"

"Dr. Simpson, I just thought I would come and see you," I replied with a flirtatious smile.

## IX

"It's so nice to see you," Dr. Simpson said, closing his laptop.

"I was in the neighborhood and I just thought I'd drop by," I replied, walking to his desk. "You know, Dr. Simpson, I never got to thank you for everything you did for me." I walked around his desk and began to rub his shoulders. "I used to see how you looked at me when I was here." I whispered in his ear.

He did think that Harlem was an attractive young lady. He had dreamed about her on numerous occasions. But sleeping with her could risk his job, his career. "Harlem, you are so beautiful," he told her. "But what is it you want from me?"

"She's very rude to me. And she has something of mine," I said, lifting my leg up and putting it on his shoulder.

He moved his head towards my lap, then he kissed my thighs. I let him taste me before I put my leg down. I kissed him, unbuckled his pants, then dropped to my knees. Seduction was my weapon, and he was now another innocent bystander. As he was about to climax from my mouth, I stood up. I hopped on top of him and rode him to the finish line.

He soon let out a passionate moan as I bounced up and down. As he threw his head back, I rolled my eyes. I was disgusted, but whatever it took to get Jenny out the picture.

"So, anything I say you'll do?" I whispered, nibbling on his ear.

"Yes. Yes, Harlem. I'll do anything for you," he replied, moving my hips back and forth.

"I want you to fire Jenny," I demanded. I stopped and looked him in the eyes.

"Jenny? Why? She's been here for 20 plus years. I can't fire her," he said, attempting to kiss me.

"Oh, you can, and you will," I said, taking the gun from my purse. I pointed to the camera that was hidden in the plant in the corner.

His eye shot open. "I … I'll do it." He gulped.

"Good boy," I said, starting to ride him again. "Now, finish." I commanded, bending over.

He pounded me for two minutes before he came inside of me. With no more time to waste, I showed him the video of Jenny and Juelz, fucking. I then gave him a rundown on how it was going to go.

"Do nothing until you get the call from me," I said, walking towards the door.


He reluctantly nodded, aware that he had no other choice but to oblige. If not, she would destroy his career and his marriage.

# X

"Good morning, beautiful," Juelz said, kissing her on the cheek. "Last night was amazing."

Jenny looked at him, smiled, then rolled on top of him. "Amazing you are," she said. "And for that, I love you."

"How about round two?" he asked, kissing her neck.

"I wish," she chuckled. "I have to shower and go see Dr. Simpson about Harlem." She rolled off him and walked to the bathroom. "But you can get me some coffee going." She looked back and smiled.

After she closed the bathroom door, Juelz got up, put on his robe, and went to the kitchen.


"Good morning handsome," a voice called out.

When he turned around, he was started by who he saw. I was sitting at the table with my legs crossed. My black sheer lingerie was revealed under my trench coat. His eyes widened as he admired my body. He knew it was wrong. But he was captivated.

"Go put some clothes on, now," he said, walking to the coffee machine.

"Why? Don't you love my body?" I asked, walking to him.

"Harlem, for the last time, I'm getting married. It's nothing between us anymore," he said.

I pressed up against him and noticed that he was beginning to harden.

"Kiss me. You know you want to," I tempted.

He deeply wanted to, but he had to stay strong. "No, Harlem. No more," he rejected.

I ignored him and pressed against him harder. "Do you miss me?" I whispered in his ear.

I took his hands and put them on my ass. He started to squeeze it, as only he could.

I then kissed his neck. "I love you, Juelz."

I lifted my leg beside him, resting my feet on the counter behind him. As I stood in front of him, he gave in, and kissed me back. I grabbed *him* and rubbed *him* on my clitoris.

"Where's Jenny?" I moaned.

"Shower, getting ready for work," he grunted.

I released *him*, put my leg down, and backed away.

"When she leaves, come see me," I said, closing my robe.

As I turned the corner, I bumped into her. "Oh! Jenny, good morning," I said, walking away.


Jenny continued to watch Harlem until she entered the kitchen. "When did she get here?" she asked.

"How would I know? I've been with you," Juelz replied, turning his back to her.

"I'm leaving for work. I love you," she said, walking to him. She kissed him on the cheek and left the house.


*Knock. Knock.*

"Harlem?" he asked, opening the door.

When he entered, I was laying on the bed, my bare body on full display. Juelz smiled, dropped his robe, then walked to the bed. He climbed on top of me, entered me slowly, then began to stroke. We made love like never before. The undeniable love was there, although he knew it was wrong.

*Knock. Knock.*

"Jenny, I'm glad to see you. Please come in," Dr. Simpson said as Jenny opened the door.

She walked to his desk and took a seat.

"I came to talk to you about Harlem," she rushed.

"Jenny, before you begin. I have to say something."

"This can't wait?"

He opened his laptop, and showed Jenny the video of her and Juelz. "I'm sorry, Jenny. We have to let you go."

"What? This is crazy!" she shouted, jumping from the chair. "Harlem is behind this! If you let me explain."

"Jenny, this got back to our biggest client. I fought for you. But this is a business, nothing personal," he explained.

Jenny stood and walked out of the office with her head held high. Harlem was taking everything from her. Her dignity, she had to keep. When she entered her car, she couldn't stop the tears from falling. She has been with that company for over 20 years.

*Beep. Beep.*

When she opened the message, the video stunned her. The attached message said,

*YOU WON'T WIN!*

"Get your ass up!" Jenny yelled, bombarding into the bedroom, where Juelz was sleeping

"Jenny! What are you doing home?" he asked surprised, sitting up.

She leaped to a drawer and pulled out her pistol. "Are you fucking kidding me!" she shouted, throwing her phone at him. "Get your shit and get the hell out of my house!"

He looked at the phone and his heart dropped. "Jenny! Baby, please, let me tell you what happened! It's not what you think."

*Cock.*

"You have five seconds to get your shit and leave. Before I put five rounds in you," she promised.

She wanted to hear what he had to say. Her intuition told her that he was under Harlem's control. But today was just not the fucking day.

Juelz hurried to put on his clothes, packed an overnight bag, and headed to the door. "If you'd just let me explain. Please!" he begged.

She didn't speak, just continued to point the gun at him. He knew that she was serious, so he turned and walked away.

She locked the door behind him, fell to the floor, and began to weep. *What seemed like the perfect love story somehow turned into a love nightmare,* she thought.

"Every since Ms. Harlem came into my house. I'm not gone let this bitch come take what's mine," she declared out loud. She dried her eyes, stood up, then lifted her gun. "Harlem! Where are you!" She yelled, walking towards the guestroom.

It was either kill or be killed.

"Harlem! I know you're in this house!" she screamed, leaving out of the guestroom.

Jenny had always been a calm spirit. This was the first time she'd ever been full of anger and rage. The first time she'd seen *red.*

"Harl—"

*Bam!*

## XII

"Juelz! What … are you … doing?" Jenny, struggled to say, fighting to free her wrists from the chair. "Why do you have me tied up? Let me go!"

"I can't do that, Jenny," Juelz said, sitting across from her on the bed. He suddenly stood and began pacing back and forth. "I tried to tell you. But you didn't listen to me. I told you she was crazy. I told you to send her back. But you didn't listen. Instead, you kept her ass in this house. You made it so hard for me."

"Juelz, please, just let me go. We can talk about this. I know it wasn't you. I believe you," Jenny cried.

He stared at her intensively. He wanted to let her go, he did love her. But right then, he was under Harlem's spell, and he couldn't let Jenny hurt her.

"Juelz, please!" she begged.

"I can't let you hurt her!" he shouted, pointing the gun to her face.

Jenny eyes widened, as she looked down the barrel of betrayal. She couldn't believe the man that said he loved her, turned his back on her. She knew that Harlem's hold was powerful, just not how powerful it was.

"Juelz, I'm not going to hurt her," she promised. "I'm going to get her the help she needs."

Juelz continued to stare at her blankly. Tears began to fall from her eyes as he cocked the gun. He knew what he was doing was wrong, but he had to protect Harlem.

"Juelz! Please! I love you! I'm going to be your wife!" she yelled, attempting a final Hail Mary.

Those words were like a snap of two fingers. Awakening him from being hypnotized. He dropped the gun, fell to Jenny's knees, and began to weep.

"Jenny, I'm sorry. Please forgive me," he begged.

"Shhh. I understand and it's okay. We're going to be okay. I need to go see Dr. Simpson, now!"

Juelz started to untie her, but stopped suddenly. He kissed her passionately, before he went to finish untying her. But before he could finish, he was interrupted.

*Cock.*

"Nobody fucking move," a voice said calmly.

## XIII

"Harlem!" Juelz said, standing up quickly.

"You just couldn't do it. Could you?" I said, pointing the gun at them. "She has to die. That's the only way we can be together! All you had to do was pull the damn trigger!"

"Har—" Juelz started to say.

"Shut up!" I yelled, walking over to Jenny.

Jenny began to cry when I put the gun to her head. "Please, Harlem. I'll give anything you want. Just don't kill me," she begged.

"Hahaha!" I laughed. "You see Jenny, I'm not going to kill you. He is." I said, looking at Juelz.

He began to sweat profusely, and his heartbeat increased. "Harlem, please don't do this," he pleaded.

"Pick up the gun and put it to her head," I instructed.

He obliged.

"You see. This is what happens when you take what's mine!" I said, staring deep into her eyes. "You pay the fucking price, you bitch." I stepped back and pointed my gun at Juelz. "Shoot her or I'll kill you."

"Harlem, please! She didn't take me. I'm with you," Juelz lied.

"No! No! No! I want her dead! Now, kill her or I'll kill the both of you!" I yelled. As I looked at Juelz, he looked at Jenny. "Pull the damn trigger now!"

*Bam!*

Jenny kicked me in the leg, causing me to crash to the floor. I rushed to grab the gun just as Juelz went for it.

"Harlem, stop! Give me the gun," he demanded as we wrestled for it.

We rolled around on the ground for a few seconds before,

*Pow! Pow!*

## XIV

## The Finale

"Baby! No! No! Get up! Please!" I screeched at Juelz, applying pressure to his gunshot wound.

I tugged on him to help him up; he cried out in pain. As we slipped to the floor from his blood, Jenny looked on petrified.

"Bitch! This is all your fault!" I said, standing and pointing the gun at her.

"My fault?" Jenny chuckled. "How is this my fault? You're a twisted delusional bitch!" She snapped.

"Don't talk to me that way!"

"Harlem, please call the ambulance for him. He's bleeding everywhere! Please save him!" she begged.

"So they can call the police? I'm not going back to that place, Jenny! I'm not! Why didn't you just leave him alone! You just had to have him! Didn't you? He belongs to me! I should have killed you when I had the chance."

*Cock.*

"Harlem, please!" Juelz grunted through blood.

"Baby! I'm sorry!" I said, dropping to my knees beside him. "You should have let go of the gun. I'm sorry, my love, but I must kill her. That's the only way we can be together." I concluded, turning towards Jenny with my finger on the trigger.

When I saw her, my heart dropped.

"Goodbye, bitch!"

*Pow! Pow! Pow!*

I

## Chanel And Victor

"Chanel! Chanel! Hurry up, slow poke! They're about to start playing," Quay shouted.

Quay was my oldest sister and my best friend. My middle sister was Kendra, but we were not as close. My name's Chanel. I lived in East Brooklyn with my parents and two sisters. My father was a pastor and my mother was a high paid attorney. It was the summer after my high school graduation and I was ready to break loose and be free. This day, I would do that by watching the basketball game and *him.*

His name was Victor, the most handsome man I'd ever seen. He was a drug dealer, which only attracted me to him even more. He would glance at me often, but we had never spoken.

"You think Victor will be there?" I asked Quay, as we walked onto the porch.

"He's always there. But don't get too happy. He never speaks to you," she chuckled.

"Well, he's going to speak today," I smiled.


When we arrived, the game had already started. As we sat on the bench, my gaze went straight to Victor. I began to fantasize as the sweat dripped from his chocolate muscles. His fade emphasized his beautiful eyes and bright smile. Everywhere he went, my eyes followed.

"Stop staring! You're making it so obvious," Quay said, nudging me.

But I couldn't, I was trapped in a trance.

"Yo, ma!" a voice called out, as I snapped out of my daze. "Can you toss me the ball?"

"Huh?" I replied puzzled.

"The ball. Hand me the ball," Victor said, approaching me.

I stood from the bench and grabbed the ball, resting at my feet.

"Thanks, ma," he said, as I handed it to him. We stared into each other's eyes, captivated by the possibilities. "Hand me your phone."

When I obliged, he dialed his phone number. "Make sure you answer when I call," he demanded, handing the phone back to me.

I nodded, smiled, then walked back to the bench. Naïve to the possibility that this moment would change my life, forever.

II

It had been three weeks since I met Victor. He still hadn't called me yet, which had my mind racing.

*Ringggg.*

"Hello?" I answered, hesitant to pick up this unknown number.

"Yo, ma. What's good?" he replied.

I smiled big, like a kid on Christmas Day. "Oh, my goodness. You finally called," I said sarcastically.

"Of course, I called."

"Well, it's been weeks now. So, I wasn't sure."

"Yea, I know. I got caught up handling things. Want to get away with me for a few hours?"

My eyes lit up and my heart began to race. "Sure," I replied.

"Cool. I'll be there at 7pm. Text me your address," he requested before hanging up.


After I sent him the text, I rushed to the shower. I couldn't help but fantasize what it would be like to be Victor's girl. By the time I showered and got dressed, it was 7pm.

When I walked outside, he was waiting for me in his Escalade Truck. I wore a tight fit black dress that hugged my curves, black heels, and earrings that read, 'CHANEL'.

"Damn, ma. You doing it like that?" he laughed when I stepped into the car.

I didn't say anything, just smiled, and blushed. That night we went to dinner, took a walk, then went for dessert. He opened doors for me everywhere we went and held my hand. A true gentleman. I was in heaven.

A few hours later, we pulled back up at my house.

"I had an awesome time tonight," I blushed, unbuckling my seatbelt.

"It's plenty more where that came from, ma," he replied, leaning in, and kissing me on my forehead. "I'll never rush you. Only when you're ready."

I nodded, stepped out of the car, and watched him drive off.

When I got in the house, I went to my room, opened the door, and turned on the light.

"Where have you been, Chanel?" he asked, startling me completely.

## III

"Daddy! You scared me!" I shrieked, taking off my jacket

"Where were you, Chanel? I want answers," he said angrily.

"Daddy, I was just hanging out with a friend. Nothing that's too serious."

"Umhum," he stated, standing to walk out. "You know what you were taught. Not only are you representing God, but me as well."

"I know. I just hung out with a friend, daddy. I'm almost eighteen."

He didn't respond, just kissed my forehead, and left out. I then showered, before collapsing onto my bed.


*Buzz. Buzz.*

*I had fun with you tonight, ma. See you tomorrow.*

I smiled as chills went through my body from reading his text. I closed my eyes, imagined his dark chocolate body, then dosed off.


My mornings since that night had been amazing. I'd seen Victor every day, which was like a dream come true. He took me out and showed me to the world. He hadn't put a title on us yet, but I was his girl for sure. My parents were gone for the evening, so I had the house to myself.

"Do you want to come in?" I asked him as we pulled up to my house.

"Are you ready for that?" he asked.

I hesitated at first, but then confidently said, "Yes. Yes, I'm ready."

He turned off the car, got out, and walked around to open my door. I took his hand and led him to the front door. When we entered, we walked straight to my room.

We sat on my bed and talked for a few hours. I had to admit that I was surprised he wasn't rushing to have sex with me. But soon, he stood, and prepared to leave by kissing me.

"Wait!" I said loudly, as he opened the door. He stopped in his tracks and turned to me. "Don't go. I'm ready to give myself to you."

I removed my clothes and laid on the bed naked.

"Are you sure?" he asked, admiring my body.

"I'm sure," I confirmed.

He locked the door, removed his clothes, then walked to the bed. He climbed on top of me and spread my legs. We began kissing as he caressed my hardened nipples.

"Relax, baby. Stop shaking. I'll go slow," he assured me.

I inhaled, relaxed, and spread my legs wider. When he entered me, I let out a loud squeal. This was my first time, so it took me a minute to relax my body. But when I finally embraced the pleasure, I was all in.

"Victorrr," I moaned, pressing my nails into his back.

Twenty minutes later, I wrapped my legs around him as I climaxed. He followed my lead a few seconds later. He collapsed on me, breathing heavily.

"Are you o—"

"Chanel!" she exclaimed as she opened my door, interrupting such a beautiful moment.

IV

A few weeks passed since I'd heard from Victor. I reached out to him, but he didn't replied.

*I hope my sister didn't run him off when she walked in on us,* I thought.

I couldn't help but think about that amazing night we spent together. And amazing it was! I loved having his chocolate body on mine and inside of me.

*Buzz. Buzz.*

*I've been going through it. I need you. I'll be by to pick you up later. Be ready.*

That text from Victor instantly put a smile on my face. However, I couldn't help but imagine what he could be going through. I wanted to ask him, but I simply replied, "Okay."

A few hours later, he pulled into my driveway. I smiled at him when I stepped into the car, but he didn't smile back. He soon turned to me, grabbed my hands, and kissed me.

"I'm sorry, ma," he said, driving off.

"Where are we going? I asked.

He didn't reply, just continued to drive in silence. We soon pulled up to a house with a lot of cars outside. He got out, then walked around, and opened my door.

"Yo' Vic! Where u been?" asked a light skin man with dreads, when we entered the house.

My eyes widened with surprised by what I saw. There was money and drugs damn near to the ceiling! Various women walked around in lingerie, counting cash, and bagging drugs. He didn't introduce me to anyone, we just walked to a back room.

"Come live with me," he said, shutting the door behind him.

I looked at him with a smile, but on the inside, I was confused. He ignored me for weeks and now he wanted me to live with him?

"Victor, I ... don't know what to say," I replied.

"Just say you'll come," he said, kissing me.

"Okay, I will," I surrendered.

He grabbed my face, kissed me again, and said, "Let's go home."


We left the trap house and headed to his house. He lived far on the other side of town. We soon pulled up to a big beautiful house, with guards outside. When we entered, he gave me a quick tour, before showing me to our room.

Once there, he guided me to the bed, and removed my pants. He unbuttoned his pants, pulled *himself* out, and entered me. Sweat poured from our bodies, and the sound of love making filled the room. After we were satisfied, he put on a robe, as I continued to lay there.

*Knock. Knock.*

When he opened the door, a girl handed him some money. She looked to be my age, maybe a little older.

"This it?" he asked her.

*Slap!*

"Bitch, where's the rest of my money!" he screamed, grabbing her by the throat. "Bring me my money! I don't care if you have to be out all night. Or I will kill you."

My eyes shot open, realizing that he was a pimp.

V

"Who was that?" I asked, shaking uncontrollably.

"Business," he replied.

His eyes were red, and I was scared. I started to think that I might have made a mistake. But I was afraid to tell him that I wanted to go home.

"Chanel, you have to understand. I own a business. I just like things right," he said, grabbing my face. "Just do as I say, and everything will be good."

Weeks passed since I'd moved in with Victor. I hadn't left his house since then. I went home to pack some clothes a few days after that. But that was it. I started out counting money made by the working girls. I was in the middle of counting when I received a text.

Buzz. Buzz.

*Chanel, we're worried about you. Please call us.*

It was from Quay. I did miss my family and my home, but I was in too deep. A few days ago, Victor introduced me to the corner. He said that it would help bring money into the house. And I did anything to see him happy. I found out the hard way the consequence of not doing so.

"Ma, I need you tonight," Victor said, walking into the kitchen.

"Victor, I'm tired. Is there no one else? Please?" I asked.

*Slap!*

As soon as I hit the floor, he grabbed my throat. "Obviously, there's someone else. But I told you! Now, go get dressed," he demanded.

I rushed to the bedroom and slammed the door behind me. I walked into the bathroom and stared at my reflection. The black eye and busted lip made me unrecognizable to myself. I began crying as I turned the water on and stepped in the shower.

Afterwards, I got dressed, and applied makeup. Before I left out, I removed a small bag from my purse. I poured out the white powder and snorted it. I started doing cocaine with Victor to help calm my nerves while I worked.

When I arrived at the corner, I was tired, but alert. I began strolling the street, looking for a low life to fuck. If I didn't bring home my quota, Victor would be enraged, and I would have to pay for it. One way or the other. A car pulled to the curb soon after, and he was interested in my services. Just as I was about to step into his car, I heard a voice that I was too familiar with.

"Chanel! Chanel! Is that you?" she called out.

## VI

I looked up and there stood my sister, Quay. She looked at me with pity and disbelief. I closed the car door and began to walk fast down the street.

"Chanel! Please, wait!" she yelled, following behind me.

Suddenly, I stopped and turned around. I looked at my sister, tears filling our eyes.

"What happened to you?" she asked, rubbing my face. "Come home. We can help you!" She promised, holding out her hand.

I desperately wanted to reach for her and go home. Instead, I wiped my tears. "I'm grown now, Quay. I have my own life to live. And Victo—"

"Victor?" she asked, interrupting me. "Victor got you doing this shit? Chanel, wake up! He doesn't love you!"

"Stop it! Yes, he does. Look, this is my life. Let me live it. I'm doing fine," I lied.

I hugged my sister and walked away. When I looked back, she was still standing there, with tears in her eyes.

Oh, how I wanted to run to my sister and go home. But I loved Victor. Besides, I truly believed that if I did, he would find me and kill me. As I continued to walk, I turned a few corners, creating distance between us. I snorted some cocaine and got back to work.

I made the most money out of all the girls. Not only that, but Victor and I went out from time to time. And he gave me some of the money that I made. I was still his girl and he still loved me.

I got back to the house around 2 that morning. I was exhausted, but at least all the money was made. I was just ready to shower and lay down next to my man.

"Victor, I'm home!" I yelled, walking to the bedroom, still buzzed from the drugs. "Vic, honey? Did you hear me?" I asked, opening the bedroom door. I turned the lights on, and I was shocked by what I saw. "What the hell!" I screamed.

## VII

"Go get your clothes on and leave me with Chanel," Victor directed the girl in the bed.

She gathered her clothes and walked towards the door. Before she walked out, she teased, "You're not the only one that can have Victor." She chuckled and walked out of the door.

"How could you? My sister?" I snapped, after the door closed behind her.

*Slap!*

Before I touched the ground, he grabbed my throat.

"First off, realize who the hell you talking to. Next time, I'll break your fucking jaw," he threatened, before throwing me on the ground.

When he left the room, I continued to lay there. I was hurt by the pain of his hands and by betrayal. No, Kendra wasn't my real sister. My parents adopted her before I was born. But betrayal was betrayal. It was at that moment that I realized, enough was enough. I missed my home and my parents. But most of all, I missed Quay. I stood up, grabbed my phone, and texted her. I told her that I was ready to come home. She replied, telling me to meet her.

I packed a bag and crept to the door. When I reached it, I ran out as if I had nothing else to lose. When I reached the corner store, Quay was there waiting for me. When I walked up, she grabbed me, and hugged me tight.

"I can't let mama and daddy see me this way. Please let's get a room," I begged.

We got in the car and drove to a hotel. While there, I began telling her about Victor and Kendra. She couldn't help looking at my bruises and my black eyes.

"How come you le—"

"Shhh, not right now. Please don't lecture me," I interrupted. She obliged and hugged me.

I dosed off quickly as my body was exhausted. She cuddled up to me like she did when we were younger. I felt safe and it was good being with her. But I had to admit, part of me was missing Victor. Yes, he had a temper at times, but I was still his woman. And that's where I belonged. I gingerly got up from the bed, got dressed, and wrote a note.

*'I love you Quay. And I've missed you more than life. But I miss Victor and my home. Please understand. I love you.'*

I put the note on the table, took $500 from her purse, and left out. If I had money to give to Victor, he'd think I was out working. Not intending to flee from him. I called an Uber and walked to the gas station on the corner to wait.

When I arrived home, Victor was still asleep. "I love you," I whispered in his ears. I got into bed and held him from behind.

## VIII

When I woke up, I turned over to retrieve my phone. I had over twenty missed calls from Quay. I hated betraying her trust and love. But Victor was my drug that I was not ready to get over. A few minutes later, he woke up.

"Good morning, beautiful," he smiled.

He spread my legs and inserted two fingers into my love box. I closed my eye, embracing each thrust. Just as I was about to come, he removed his fingers and climbed on top of me.

"Victorrr," I moaned.

The harder his strokes got, the louder I moaned. A few pleasurable moment later, we climaxed together. He collapsed on top of me, as we continued to lay there. I could feel the rhythm of his heartbeat against my skin.

I embraced the melody until he kissed me and rolled out of bed. "I have some business to take care of this weekend," he said, walking into the bathroom. "I'm leaving you in charge of the girls."

"You're leaving me in charge?" I asked dubiously.

"I love you. I trust you can you handle it. Right?"

"Yes, I can handle it," I assured him.


Victor left the house a few hours ago. I was now in charge of his girls and his money.

*Knock. Knock.*

"Come in," I directed.

"Hey, are you sending me out?" she asked me.

I picked up the pocket notebook and glanced over it. I had written down the schedules of the girls, along with their quotas.

"No, not tonight. But you can hang with me if you want to," I replied.

Michelle was younger than me. She was 16, with bright light skin. She stood 5'5, with silky black hair that surpassed her plump breasts. I had to admit, I've been smitten since I first saw her. She didn't reply to my invite, just closed the door behind her. Since I was already cooking spaghetti, I fixed her a plate.

"Can I ask you something?" she asked as we sat at the table.

"Sure, go ahead," I replied.

"How does it feel to be sleeping with Victor? I mean ... you're like number one."

Initially, I was puzzled. But I smiled, and said, "It's worth it."

We then began talking about ourselves. Where we were from, etc. I placed the dishes in the sink before we headed to the bedroom.

Once there, I removed a small tray from the nightstand. There was a small hill of cocaine on it. I formed a line and sniffed it.

"Have you ever?" I asked her, holding up the tray.

She nodded her head 'no'.

"You want to try?" I smiled.

"Why not?" she replied.

I taught her how to snort and she seemed to enjoy it. We sniffed a few more lines, then walked to the bed. When we sat down, she leaned over, and kissed me. I moved back, looking confused.

"I'm sorry ... I didn't mea—"

She was interrupted when I leaned in and kissed her back. We laid down as we continued to kiss. She moved down to my nipples and began sucking on them. I inserted my fingers into her, as she inserted her fingers into me. We were both high as a kite, enjoying the moment. Once we climaxed, we crawled under the sheets and dosed off.

## IX

What started off as two days, turned into two weeks. Victor was still gone and I was still running the show. I couldn't lie, the power got to me. Michelle had been clinging to me, but I enjoyed her company. Someone to lay next to at night and party with. I, Chanel, was on cloud nine and I didn't expect to be anything less.

*Ringggg.*

"Hello?" I answered the unknown number.

"How's business? You taking care of home?" the voice asked. I then recognized that it was Victor.

"Of course. I told you, I got us," I replied, smiling wide.

"Good. I'll be home in about two more days. My homie Brandon is going to come by and drop off a packet for me. Put it in the safe."

"Okay. I love you," I said before he hung up.

Twenty minutes later, all the girls were out, even Michelle.

*Knock. Knock.*

"You must be Brandon," I said, opening the door. In front of me stood a tall, chocolate, dread head. "Follow me."

He followed me into the house and down the hall.

"You must be Chanel?" he asked, looking down on me.

"That I am," I replied.

I didn't notice his eyes at the door. But right then, in the light, I was hypnotized. They were a light golden brown and he had dimples.

When we got to the back, we sat at the table and started to drink.

"Seems like Vic is taking good care of you," he said.

I smiled. "I take care of myself." I put my glass down, walked to him and lifted my leg in front of him. "Would you like me to take care of you too?"

"And how are you gone do that?" he smiled.

"Let me get us another drink and I'll show you," I replied.

I went to the kitchen and poured two glasses of Hennessy. I retrieved a pill from the cabinet that I placed there earlier. I put it in his drink, and stirred until it dissolved.

*Here goes nothing,* I thought.

"Now let me show you," I said, walking into the backroom.

I handed him the drink and took his hand. He shot it down as I lead him to the bedroom.

As we walked into the room, there was an evil smile on my face. I got a taste of being a boss and I refused to lose it. When we reached the bed, I threw him onto it. I unbuckled his pants, pulled down his boxers, then inserted him into my mouth. His head fell back as he enjoyed the oral sex. He was so caught up in the moment, the betrayal slipped his mind. It didn't help that he was now drowsy because of the pills.

When I noticed that he was dosing off, I stood up and got undressed. I then walked to the dresser and pressed 'RECORD' on the camera. I walked back to the bed and mounted him.

"Fuck, Chanel!" he moaned, moving my hips back and forth.

A few strokes later, he came inside of me. I climbed off him, reached in the nightstand and pulled out a pistol.

*Click. Clack.*

"Empty your pockets," I said, pointing the gun at him.

"What the hell are you doing?" he asked, dosing in and out.

"Give me everything you have. Now!" I shouted, walking to the camera. "I'd hate to show everyone you're sleeping with Victor's girl and betraying him."

He was more alert now as he emptied his pockets.

"Now, forget about Victor. You work for me now. You'll deliver all the packets to me. Do that and Victor will never find out about this."

"Whatever, ma. You won't get away with this for too long," he said, buckling his pants.

"Get your shit and leave," I demanded, pointing the gun at him.

"I'll get away with more than you think. It's time to take Victor out," I said to myself, following him to the front door.

# X

## The Finale

Two days later, Victor returned home. All the girls were out working, so I met him at the door in my robe.

"Hello, baby! I'm so glad you're home," I said, welcoming him in and taking his bags.

"How was business while I was away?" he asked, as we walked to the bedroom.

"Good. Very good," I replied.

"Nothing interesting happened?" he asked, turning to look at me.

*What is he trying to get at?* I thought.

"Nope. Just regular business," I replied.

"Well, you must be tired," he said when we walked into the room.

"A little. But I handled everything like you asked," I replied, sitting on the bed.

He closed the door, walked to me, and took my slippers off. He began rubbing my feet and worked his way up to my thighs. Then, he stopped. I looked confused as our eyes locked. I instantly saw anger in them that made the hairs on the back of my neck stand at attention.

*Slap!*

I grabbed my face as he squeezed my thighs tightly. Suddenly, he grabbed my hair and wrapped it around his fist.

"Victor! What are you doing?" I asked, screaming for my life.

"I asked you did anything happen while I was away! And you lied to me," he screamed, slinging me to the floor.

He walked over to a cabinet by the tv and opened it with a key. I never knew what was in it, until that moment.

"See, before I left, something told me that you would betray me. So, I installed a camera!"

"Please let me explain!" I begged, as I watched myself fucking Michelle and Brandon.

He grabbed my hair again, yanked me to my feet and threw me onto the bed.

"Since you like to give it up so easy, strip now!" he demanded.

Without hesitating, I stood and took off my clothes. He then pushed me onto the bed and forced my legs apart. He entered into me violently and began jabbing in and out. I began to cry, and the more I did, the harder he pounded me. When I screamed out in pain, he grabbed my neck, and chocked me. The more I screamed, the tighter he squeezed. As he was coming, he pulled out, and squirted all over my face and body. He even pissed on me afterwards! As I laid there weeping, he punched me repeatedly in my face.

"I bet you'll think twice about playing me again! Now, go shower!" he shouted, throwing me on the floor.


I ran into the bathroom and locked the door behind me. I looked in the mirror; I couldn't recognize myself. I turned the shower on, stepped in, and broke down crying. Blood poured down the drain. As weak as I was, I tried to hold myself up.

I began singing, "I need thee, o, I need thee, every hour, I need thee."

I

## Dakota And Ronnie

"You have one-minute remaining," the automated voice said, signaling that it is time to say our goodbyes.

"I love you, Dakota. Just keep holding me down. Our love is going to expand into something great," he promised.

"I love you too, Dre," I replied, before hanging up.

A thirty-minute call every other day wasn't enough.

As you heard, my name is Dakota Brown. An 18-year-old, recent high school graduate. But most importantly, I was a mother to my three-month-old, DreKyla. And yes, she was named after her daddy, Dre. We had been together for two years. He was arrested six months ago on drug and gun charges. Since we've been together, I've never wanted for anything. I definitely never had to work. But now, my daughter needed me to make a way and so did he. I was determined to hold them down no matter what.

"Dakota, don't break bad on me," he said often.

It wasn't that he questioned my loyalty. He just knew that these streets were a dirty game.

*Ringggg.*

"Hello?" I answered.

"Kota, it's me, Bre," my best friend said.

"What's up?" I replied.

"Stanley asked are you coming in tonight? It's supposed to be mad ballers."

"Ballers? Hell, yea! Let me drop Kyla off at my momma house. I'm on the way."

Bre and I worked *at Blue Magic Gents Joint*. Yea, I know what you're probably thinking. I was a typical young, single, black mother. That was far from the facts. But I had people depending on me, my daughter the most important.

"Okay, don't be late. Doors open at 8pm," she said.

After we hung up, I showered, then got us dressed.

Shortly later, I dropped Kyla off, and pulled up at the club. Stanley had been letting me dance and make money there since I was sixteen.

"You're young but your body sure damn not," he said the day he hired me.

And he was absolutely right. I had curves, hips, and an ass. And let's not forget my perky breasts and full lips. I still did. When I walked in, the VIP area was already blocked off. That's where I usually made my money.

"Hey! You're finally here!" Bre said, walking out in her g string and bra.

"Who's supposed to be here tonight?" I asked as we walked to the locker room.

"That dude Ronnie and his boys," she smiled, looking in the mirror.

We had heard about Ronnie. He was a big-time drug dealer from Miami. *I wonder what he's doing in LA,* I thought.

After I changed into my lingerie, I went and stood behind the curtains. "Welcome to the stage, Miss Coca Kota!" The Dj shouted into the mic.

When I stepped onto the stage, I became another person. There was nothing there but me and the pole. I climbed to the top, twirled by my legs, then dropped into a split. I blacked out the music and my movements, only focusing on the bills falling to my feet.

After my show, I went to the dressing room, dripping in sweat.

"Kota, you killed it out there tonight! You racked up," Bre cheered, walking in behind me. "Ronnie is asking for you, *by name*."

"Me?" I asked shocked. "Okay. Let me clean up."

I washed off, fixed my hair, grabbed my robe, then walked to the VIP area.

"Here she is," Bre said, as we walked up.

"Hi, I'm—"

"Shhh, ma," he interrupted "We know who you are. You're the reason we came here. Come sit by me." He gestured.

That was a moment that would change my life for better or for worse.

## II

"Y'all came to see me?" I asked Ronnie, walking towards him.

"Yea. We heard you're the Queen here. Everybody want to see you, Kota," he replied.

I smiled, as I was captivated by his intoxicating grey eyes.

As I got lost in them, he smiled. "Let me take you to get something to eat. The room service is great where I'm at."

I was hesitant at first for numerous reasons. One, was because of Dre, whom I loved. Two, was the risk of losing my family. And three, the most obvious, I just met this man.

"I ... I don't know," I said shyly. "I have more dancing to do. Plus, Stanley isn't going to let me leave. Not with a crowd like this." I looked at Stanley, who just walked into the VIP area.

"It's cool. He gave you the night off," Ronnie said, walking up to Stanley. He handed him a rubber band of cash. He then looked back at me. "Come on, cutie."

He held out his hand, which I stood, and grabbed confidently. As we walked out, I smiled at Bre', assuring her that I would be okay.

"Relax and make yourself at home," Ronnie said as we entered his suite.

My eyes wondered around the presidential suite, stopping suddenly at the window. I opened the balcony door and stepped outside, mesmerized by the city lights. The view of the river was just as beautiful.

*I can get used to this,* I thought.

He grabbed my hand, walked me back into the room, then asked, "Do you have anybody special in your life?"

I nervously looked at the ground as my heart began to race. I couldn't help but to think what Dre would say if he knew I was there. But it was just dinner, right?

"My baby daddy. But he's in prison right now," I said.

"Kids?" he asked, twirling me around.

"A daughter," I blushed.

"Kota, let me take care of you and your daughter," he said, holding my hands in his, looking down at me.

"Ronnie, you don't know me," I chuckled, releasing his hands.

"I know more than you think," he said, removing a stack of money from his pocket, sitting in on the table. "Here."

"Ronnie, I can't take this," I said, scooting it towards him.

"Enjoy it, on me. It's plenty more where that came from," he said, walking to the dresser. He retrieved a jewelry box, walked back to the table and placed it in front of me. "Open it."

I was reluctant but opened it anyways. It was the most beautiful white gold necklace I'd ever seen.

"Ronnie!" I screamed. "I can't take this. It's too much."

He walked behind me and placed it around my neck. He walked me to the mirror. "You're gorgeous. You deserve it."

"Thank you," I replied, admiring my reflection.

"Now, let me take care of you," he said.

## III

I slept peacefully in Ronnie's arms last night. Surprisingly, he didn't try to have sex with me. I respected him for that. He just held me all night. He recently dropped me off at home. I'm now laying on the couch, staring at the necklace he gifted me. For a moment, I pictured what life could be like with him in Miami. My imagination was interrupted when phone started vibrating.

"Yes," I answered.

"You have a prepaid call fro—"

I cut off the automated voice, pressing 1.

"Hello?" I said, sitting up.

"Yo! Where the fuck you been? I've been calling you," Dre snapped.

"Dre, I'm sorry. I was out with Bre last night. We had a girl's night," I replied.

I hated lying to him, but if he knew I was dancing again, he would kill me. Let alone spent the night with another man.

"Man, don't let that shit happen again. When I call, you pick up," he demanded.

Dre was a sweet man; but he was also controlling and demanding. It was always about what he wanted and how he wanted it.

"Dakota, do you hear me?"

*Enough was enough!*

"Dre! Shut the fuck up!" I screamed. "All you do when you call is bitch! I'm out here holding shit down by myself!" I paused and took a deep breath. "Look, we need to take some time."

"Time? What do you mean time, Dakota? I might not have much time left."

He was referring to the fact that his lawyer was working to get him released on bond. If it was denied *again*, he would be incarcerated until his trial. *Whenever that may be.*

"Dre, you make me feel so unappreciated. You don't know what I'm dealing with out here without you," I cried. "It's hard enough that you got arrested while I was pregnant. Then, left me to give birth alone, to be a single mother. Kyla has to be without a father for now. I can't handle this stress."

By this point, my sadness had fled. I was now fully enraged and absolutely over it.

"Besides, I met someone last night."

"What?" he asked, as if he didn't hear me the first time.

"You heard me, Dre," I replied, tempted to hang up.

"You met who?" he snapped.

"It doesn't matter. I need time to thi—"

"You have one-minute remaining," the automated voice interrupted.

"Dakota? You're going to do me like this while I'm in here?"

"Dre, I'm sor—"

I flopped back onto the couch after the call disconnected. Tears fell from my eyes and steam blew from my ears. I loved Dre and he was my whole world, besides my daughter. He was there when I had nobody. But he wasn't there now, and now is when I need him.

*Knock. Knock.*

"Come in!" I shouted, wiping my face.

"Where you been, hot mama?" Bre asked, with a slick smile, walking in.

"Ronnie took me to his suite. Girl, it was beautiful," I said, forcing the Dre situation out of my mind.

"Ohhh! You slept with him! Didn't you?" she assumed.

"No, he was a complete gentleman," I blushed. "He wants us to move to Miami with him. I already told Dre that we needed some space."

Her eyes widened with shock. They had been best friends since grade school. It was Bre that introduced us, two years ago.

"What am I going to do?" I asked her.

"That's something you have to figure out. Now what about Dre?" she asked.

"I don't know, Bre. He's putting too much stress on me. Besides, Ronnie gave me this," I said, handing her the jewelry box.

"Wow!" she said, mesmerized by the expensive jewelry. "Well, you better figure it out! And figure it out fast!"

"I will. I wouldn't mind trying out the Miami life," I replied as she handed it back to me.

"I feel you, boo. Well, I have to go meet someone. Love ya," she said, heading out the door.


After she closed the door behind herself, I opened the jewelry box. I gazed at the necklace, smiled, then pulled out my phone to text him.

*I'm ready to see the Miami life.*

IV

The Finale


A few days had passed since I sent that fateful text. I told him that Bre and I would come visit Miami. I was seriously thinking about moving there with him. But first, I needed to go see what it was like. My mother was keeping Kyla for the weekend, so I packed in peace. I was upset that I was probably going alone though. I had been calling Bre for the last few days, but nothing. I mean, I could go by myself, I would had just loved to have my girl with me.


Meanwhile,

"I have to come, Ronnie. If not, she's not going come," the voice said. "And I told you to just come swoop her off her feet. Why do you want to move her to Miami?"

*Slap!*

"Bitch! Don't you question me! Or I'll break your damn jaw!" he threatened. "Now, if she would like you to go, call her and tell her you're coming. I'll have the limo meet y'all at the airport. Pick up the tickets and get y'all asses on the plane." He grabbed her by the face and kissed her. "Don't worry, Bre. You're still my number one." He said before walking away.

Bre then took out her phone and called Dakota.


*Ringggg.*

"Hey! Where you been? I've been calling you!" I said as soon as I answered.

"I'm sorry, boo. I've been sick. But I got your message and of course I'll go with you," Bre replied.

"Oh, yay! I'm so excited. He just texted and said our tickets are ready. Meet me here."

"Okay, I'll see you soon," she responded before hanging up.


When the call was disconnected, Bre continued to sit in deep thought. She was irritated by Ronnie, but pleased that her plan was in motion.

"I have to get a message to Dre," she declared to herself.

She picked up her phone and texted her cousin. He was a prison guard where Dre was locked up. The message was to have Dre call her from the cell.

"Once I tell him this, and have the pictures for proof, I will finally have him. I can get rid of both Ronnie and Dakota. DreKyla was supposed to be mine anyways. She doesn't even spend time with her," Bre smirked, walking to her room to start packing.


Soon, we arrived at the airport. The tickets were waiting for us just as Ronnie had promised. We checked in, went through security, then boarded the plane.

"Let's go have some fun!" I said with utter excitement. "I'm glad I'm sharing this experience with my best friend." I said, hugging Bre.

"Me too, boo," she responded, taking the window seat. "Let the fun begin."

About The Author:


Whitney E. Sawyer was born on August 23, 1989 in Knoxville, TN. She graduated from Austin East Magnet High School, and attended Pellississippi State Community College. She is the mother of two wonderful sons Jaylen (11) and ZaCari (1). "The Secrets That Lies Between: A Collection Of Erotic Short Stories" is her debut book with aspirations to publish more.

## Acknowledgements:

First, I want to give God all the praise and honor for blessing me with this lovely talent. To my wonderful parents for bringing me into this world. To my sisters in LOVE, Tachae and Jamithia for always pushing and uplifting me when I needed it the most. And to my wonderful Publisher, Chanekka Pullens, words can't begin to express my love and gratefulness towards you. Thank you for seeing something in me and helping to make my dreams come true!

I LOVE YOU ALL!

www.ingramcontent.com/pod-product-compliance
Lightning Source LLC
Chambersburg PA
CBHW070030260626
47159CB00005B/2001